Kaitty Lorenz: New Life

Mysti J. Rolenc

Copyright © 2011 by Mysti Rolenc

Kaitty Lorenz
New Life
by Mysti Rolenc

Printed in the United States of America

ISBN 9781613798546

All rights reserved solely by the author. The author guarantees all contents are original and do not infringe upon the legal rights of any other person or work. No part of this book may be reproduced in any form without the permission of the author. The views expressed in this book are not necessarily those of the publisher.

Unless otherwise indicated, Bible quotations are taken from The Adventure Bible NIV. Copyright © 2000 by Zonderkidz.

www.xulonpress.com

Dedicated to

*My awesome family,
For sticking beside me and encouraging me*

*And to my best friend,
Who's given me so many ideas that have helped
create this story!*

"For the wages of sin is death, but the gift of God is eternal life in Christ Jesus our Lord."
Romans 6:23

Chapter One

Kaitty Lillian Carmichael sat huddled in heavy blankets on the couch of her living room watching TV. It was Christmas and she was alone. She had no place to go for Christmas, not a relative or friends' house. She had gone to the church services that morning, but then was alone the rest of the day. She had been told that she was welcome to come to her boyfriend's house, but she didn't want to intrude while he and his family had their celebration. He and his family were the only friends she had. She had had others, but they no longer talked.

Kaitty thought the show on TV was stupid, but there was nothing else on when she looked last. She flipped through the channels, looking for anything else. She finally found a channel that showed a Christmas movie; The Nativity Story.

There was a knock on the door. She wondered who it could be. She looked to the clock on the wall; it read eleven o'clock. Who would be out and about that late?

She took caution. She grabbed a bat that sat in the corner by the door and slowly opened it, peaking through the inch gap of the opened door. There she saw a tall, handsome young man standing before the door, shivering in the cold winter night.

"Edmund," she said as she opened the door, permitting him in. "What are you doing here?"

He shivered as she closed the door. He hung up his coat and they walked into the living room.

Kaitty looked up into Edmund's face of uneasiness and asked, "Why aren't you at home? Is everything okay?"

"Everything's fine," he answered.

"Then why are you here?" she asked, looking puzzled by him.

He started pacing in front of her, looking stressed and nervous. He started to mutter things to himself, just loud enough for her to hear. *"Come on! Just do it!"* he said to himself.

He stopped pacing, turned to Kaitty, and walked up to her. "Kaitty, I can't take this boyfriend/girlfriend relationship any longer." She was startled. He got down on one knee, took her hand, and continued. "Kaitty, I've been waiting for this moment for a long time—." He rummaged through his coat pocket, pulled out a small, blue box, and said, "Will you marry me?" then opened the box to reveal a beautiful small diamond ring.

Kaitty was taken aback. She began to tear up at the realization of what was happening. "Yes," she said in joy and tears.

Edmund put the ring on her finger, stood up, and she jumped into his arms. They kissed.

When they finally let go, Kaitty said, "I love you."

"I love you, too, babe. Why do you think I asked you to marry me?" And they kissed again.

He led Kaitty over to the couch and they sat and watched the rest of the movie together. It ended at half-past eleven and he told her that he needed to get home.

"Would your parents still be up?" she asked.

"I don't know," he answered. "My sister's been under the weather. They might be up taking care of her."

"Could we see?"

"I suppose so. I don't see any reason why not."

She turned off the TV. They grabbed their coats and headed out the door. Once out, she took the key from underneath the mat on the front step, locked the door, and shoved the key in her pocket. They jumped into his car and drove off to his parents' house.

The ride was mostly silence, until Kaitty asked, "Ed, do your parents like me?"

He seemed to think on the question before he answered. "Of course they do. You're practically already family to them. Why do you ask?"

"I just wanted to know. I wouldn't want family that didn't like me."

He laughed. "Well, they like you, so you don't have to worry about that."

She smiled. *How is it that he can always make me smile?* she thought.

After five minutes driving, they came to a little white house at 369 Lincoln Avenue. Edmund quickly got out, walked around to Kaitty's door, and opened it for her. *He's such a gentleman.* She thanked him once she had stepped out. He put his arm over her shoulders and they walked up to the front door. Edmund knocked on the door and waited for it to open.

They heard footsteps and then the door unlocking. Edmund's father, Cameron Lorenz, appeared behind the door. He greeted them with open arms.

"Edmund," he said, hugging him. "Hello, Kaitty."

"Hello, Mr. Lorenz."

"Please, don't be so formal! Call me Cameron." He paused and then asked, "Do we have a celebration in order?" Edmund looked to his father, smiling, and nodded. "Well, that's terrific! Wait 'til your mom and brother find out!"

"Tyler's here?" asked Edmund. Cameron nodded. "Why?"

"He's helping Jana." Edmund grabbed Kaitty's hand and pulled her into the house. She followed him into the kitchen where they found Tyler and Edmund's mom, Christine, at the table with a half-eaten French Silk pie in the middle.

"Ed," said Tyler, who was older than Edmund. He stood and hugged Edmund. "It's been a while since I've seen you. Good to see you."

"It's good to see you too, Tyler," said Edmund.

"So, what happened? You're too happy for her to have said no."

"You heard?"

"Please, mom called me when you said you were going to ask her tonight. So, I'm going to take it that she said yes." He spoke to Kaitty. "What's wrong with you, woman?"

"Oh, Tyler, stop that!" said Christine.

"I'm just kidding, mom. Well, is that what you said, Kaitty?"

"Yes," she answered. "Edmund and I are getting married."

"Well, congratulations!" said Christine, standing up and walking over to them. She gave Kaitty a tight hug.

As they let go, Kaitty asked, "Where's Jana?"

"Oh, she's upstairs in bed. She'll be so happy to see you!"

Kaitty looked at Edmund. "You go on," he said. "I want to sit down here and talk with them for a little. I'll be up there in a few, okay?"

"Alright." She took a step toward him and kissed him. She walked through the living room and up the stairs.

She rounded the corner at the top of the stairs and took a few more steps towards the first door on her right. She stopped to listen for a moment.

Jana gave a few violent coughs. Kaitty slowly cracked the door open a bit. She looked toward the bed and noticed Jana coughed continuously. Jana sat up in bed, hand closed in a fist, and held up to her mouth.

Kaitty walked in and asked if she was alright. "Water," Jana managed. Kaitty grabbed the pitcher of water on the bedside table, poured some into a glass, and handed it to Jana, who took it slowly. She put the glass up to her mouth and drank half of it.

She handed the glass back to Kaitty and said, "Thank you. Did he ask you?"

"Ask me what?"

"Oh, you know what. Did he pop the question?"

"Yes."

"Well, what did you say?"

"Well—it's not really important what I said. Just that I'm—," Kaitty sighed, "I'm going to be your sister." She held out her left hand to show her the ring that sat there on her finger.

"Oh, Kait—," Jana began, but then she started to cough violently again. Kaitty gently pushed her backward to make her lay back down on the bed and grabbed the glass of water from the table. She tilted Jana's head up and put the glass up to her mouth. She slowly drank the rest of it.

Kaitty sat the glass down again and asked, "You okay?"

"Yeah. That happens often. But mom says I'm getting better."

"Well, you look like you are." She sat down on the edge of the bed.

"Mom took my temperature this morning and it only read one-hundred and one. Yesterday was terrible. Did you hear what happened?" Kaitty shook her head. "Mom took my temperature yesterday morning and it was one-hundred and five. They had to take me to the hospital. Dad met us there, and Edmund actually wanted to wait a few weeks to ask you to marry him. I was just strong enough to put up a fight with him about it. I told him to ask you for me. He couldn't resist doing something for me when I was in the hospital with a one-hundred and five temperature.

"I was released last night and they gave mom and dad instructions on what they needed to do. They told them that, from now on, until I'm better, they need to take my temperature every morning when I wake and every night before I go to bed."

"That's sounds like a lot to do."

"Yeah, kind of. Where's Edmund?"

"Down stairs talking to your parents and Tyler."

"You mean our parents," she corrected, pointing at Kaitty then herself. "Have you already forgotten that you're going to be part of the family?"

She laughed. "No, I haven't. I guess I'm just going to have to get used to calling them—." She stopped. What *should* she call them?

"You can call us mom and dad, if you'd like." Christine stood in the doorway. Cameron, Tyler, and Edmund stood by her.

Kaitty laughed, got up, and took a couple of long strides to Edmund. He pulled her into his arms in a tight embrace. "I love you," whispered Edmund.

"And I love you," whispered Kaitty back to him. She lifted her head to look into his face and they kissed.

"Ew!" said Tyler. "First secretive talking, then kissing! What next, you getting pregnant tomorrow?"

"Tyler!" yelled Kaitty, than she slapped him across the shoulder as hard as she could. He grabbed his shoulder and recoiled.

"What was that for?" Tyler asked.

"For being a jerk," she said, though she laughed.

"You know I'm just joking."

"Well, I've gotten sick of it, Tyler," said Edmund. "Ever since I was little, you've always tried to be funny by making those stupid jokes. That will really hurt someone one day, and it might just be you. I sometimes wonder how Emma puts up with it."

"Well, she quite enjoys them! At least she thinks I'm funny."

"Ignore him, Ed," said Kaitty.

"Yes, dear, and I think it's time for you to get home."

"Why?" asked Kaitty. Edmund held up his watch to her. Kaitty looked at the time. "What! It's almost twelve-thirty!"

"So that's why I'm getting so tired and joking around!" said Tyler, yawning.

"Well, then, you two get off to bed," said Cameron to Tyler and Jana. "And you two better get going. Kaitty needs to get some sleep."

"Goodnight, Jana," said Kaitty.

"'Night, Kaitty."

"'Night, everyone," said Edmund.

They walked back down the stairs, out the door, and back into the car. As they were driving back to Kaitty's house, Edmund asked slowly, "You aren't pregnant, are you?" He looked over at her.

"Keep your eyes on the road!" yelled Kaitty.

"Sorry," he said, looking back to the road. "But you aren't, are you?"

"No, Ed, I'm not pregnant. If I was, I would've told you from the start. Don't even begin to believe what Tyler says about that."

"I know I can't trust him when he says things like that, I just wanted to make sure." Kaitty laughed.

They continued to drive for the remainder of the five minutes to Kaitty's house. When they finally arrived, she quickly hopped out of the car and waited for Edmund. He reached her, took her outstretched hand, and they walked up to the door. Kaitty dug through all of her pockets for her key. "Dang, where is it?"

"Please don't tell me you've lost your key."

"I'm sorry, but I think I have."

"Great! How are you supposed to get in?"

Kaitty looked around the front of the house. How *was* she going to get in? She spotted the window beside the door. *Of course,* she thought. *Always have to do it the hard way.*

"Ed, help me get the window open."

"What? What are you trying to do?"

"If I can get through the window, I can open the door."

He seemed reluctant, but helped push the window up. At first, it started going up fine. "I will never lock these things again," she said as she pushed. But it stopped moving when it was only half way up. "Come on, Ed. Push harder!"

They kept at it and, within a minute, they had it open. Edmund gave Kaitty a boost in, but she got stuck.

"Ed, I think my belt's caught on something!"

He took a look and sure enough, her belt was caught on a hook. "Don't move. I'll get it unhooked."

"Well, I'm not going anywhere."

Edmund fiddled with the belt, trying to get it unstuck. He finally got it and Kaitty said, "Hold on to my ankles so I can lower myself down." He did as told.

While she climbed through the window, Edmund noticed a cop car driving toward them. "Ah, Kaitty, there's a cop coming."

"So? We can identify our—." Kaitty fell into the house when Edmund let go of her feet by accident. He heard her hit the floor with a thud and something wooden falling after.

The cop noticed him and pulled his cruiser in front of the house. He stepped out of the car, stood behind the door with his gun pointed at Edmund, and yelled, "Put your hands where I can see them!"

Edmund did, and then the officer continued. "Get down on the ground!" He did. Edmund's heart was racing as he lay there, but knew it was the right thing to do. The man came over to him, hand-cuffed him, and pulled Edmund to his feet. "What were you doing? Breaking into a house on Christmas?"

"I wasn't breaking into the house. It's my fiancée's house. She lost her key so she tried to get in through the window. Her belt got stuck and I accidentally let go of her ankles once I got the belt loose. She fell inside and landed on the floor. If you look in the window she'll probably be there."

"What, unconscious?"

"Yeah. I didn't hear her move so I'm worried that she hit her head on something!"

"Like I'm going to believe that."

"Please! I think she hit her head! If she's left there, she could die! You can lock me in jail while my fiancée bleeds to death from a brain hemorrhage, but I would never forgive you or myself. Please! Set me in the car and call backup if you don't trust me, but please, I beg you, go look in there!"

The policeman took Edmund and sat him in the back of his car. He went back over to the window, stood on his toes, and looked in. He came, jogging, back to the car, got into the front seat, and called, breathlessly, over the radio to the dispatcher.

"This is Officer Scott Celter requesting fire squad and ambulance." He gave the dispatcher the address and the woman said that the fire and ambulance squads were on their way.

Minutes later, a fire truck and ambulance raced down the road, sirens blaring and lights flashing. The officer had unhand-cuffed Edmund and they led the newcomers to the scene. The firefighters busted the door open. Kaitty looked terrible as two paramedics took her to the ambulance. She had a big black and blue spot on her head and it looked like her ankle was broken because it was twisted. She was rushed to the hospital, Edmund following behind in his car.

Chapter Two

*B**eep! Beep! Beep!* Kaitty awoke. *What is that?* She slowly opened her eyes. She was staring at a white ceiling, lying in a bed. Her head throbbed, her right ankle hurt, and she was in an unfamiliar place. She looked to her left and saw a heart monitor. *That's what it was.* She looked to her right and saw a man sitting in a chair next to her, hands folded at his mouth.

Who was he? Who was she? She couldn't remember these things and was startled when the man looked up to her.

"Kaitty," he said.

She looked around the room then back to the man. "Are—are you talking to me?"

He was scared. Edmund ran out of the room and came back in with Tyler.

"Kaitty, I'm Doctor Lorenz," said Tyler. "Does this name sound familiar to you?" She shook her head. "Do you know who you are?"

She paused for a moment. "Well, I guess I'm Kaitty, since that's what you two call me."

"Do you know your last name?" She shook her head. "Do you remember anything about yourself?" She still shook her head. Then he spoke to Edmund. "I want you to tell her things. This memory loss should go away in a couple of days."

"Like how many?"

"Maybe about a week. It can vary."

"Tyler—she will remember, right?"

"It's very rare that they don't remember." He walked out of the room.

Edmund sighed and sat back down next to his fiancée. "Kaitty, what do you remember?"

"How to talk—I've just forgotten my life, not everything!"

"Okay, you remember smart remarks. Now, let's start with the basics. I'm your fiancé—."

"I'm engaged?"

"Yes, you are."

"What's your name?"

"Edmund Gabriel Lorenz. Your name is Kaitty Lillian Carmichael."

"Which spelling of Katy?"

"Not one you would remember. It's K-a-i-t-t-y—Kaitty."

"Okay, what about my family?"

There was silence. No way did he want to tell her about her family. It would be too painful, even if she couldn't remember the things that had happened. She pressed him to tell her, but he never gave in.

"Why not?" she asked.

"Because you won't be able to handle it."

"Won't be able to handle what?"

"The truth, that's what. Kaitty, you have memory loss. Once you gain back your memory, then you'll know why I couldn't tell you."

"Then what about your family? Can you tell me about them?"

"My mom's a stay-at-home mom, my dad's in the military, my little sister's sixteen, and my older brother works here as a doctor. He's the one you saw walk in."

"What religion are they?"

"Christian."

"You?"

"The same."

"Me?"

"The same. Anything else?"

"Yes, can I have something to eat?"

Edmund smiled. Even with the memory loss, Kaitty was still funny. He called in a nurse.

Kaitty asked the nurse, "Do you have chicken and noodles?"

The nurse nodded and hurried away while Edmund stared in question at Kaitty.

"How did you remember that?"

"Remember what?"

"Your favorite food—chicken and noodles. How'd you remember that?"

"I don't know. I just did, that's all."

Edmund was confused, but, if she could remember something about herself, he figured that was good.

The next day, Kaitty was released from the hospital. She and Edmund drove to his house to pack a bag. Then they drove to her house. He decided he would stay with her until her memory came back and would also make sure that she could navigate fine on crutches because she had broken her ankle from her fall through the window.

He helped her out of the car, grabbed his bags, and helped her inside. Kaitty looked around the place as if confused. She couldn't remember anything of her house; where it was, what it looked like, not even where her room was.

Edmund took her around the house and showed her where everything was. She sat down on the couch while he fixed them something to eat. She didn't know what it was, but it smelled good. Edmund came out every now and then and sat with her. About an hour later, he brought out two plates full of steaming noodles.

"What is this?" asked Kaitty.

"Chicken fettuccini. We had it on our first date. Trust me, you love it."

She shrugged and tried some. It was good. They sat and ate in silence, watching TV. Edmund wondered, *Will she ever remember everything?*

There was no progress in Kaitty's memory the rest of the week. Edmund began to worry. He took her to church that Sunday, kept her after to meet all the people again, and conferred with the pastor about her while she stood outside the office.

"Tom, I'm worried about her," Edmund told his pastor.

"Edmund, it will be fine. If God wants it this way, then it will be this way. You just have to let Him do what He thinks is best."

"But why would He let this happen? I mean, why to her?"

"I don't have an answer to everything about God, but I think He tests us in different ways. This may just be one of them. I just suggest that you pray about it."

"I have been, every day since it happened. But she couldn't even remember me! She can't remember her family and I don't have the heart to tell her about them."

"And I can see why. She's already gone through enough trauma and you don't want her to suffer the pain of knowing what her family was like. But, if God is ever tugging at your heart to tell her something, or someone else something, then do it. It may seem hard to tell someone something terrible, but, if He wants you to say it, then He'll give you the strength."

"I hope you're right."

"Believe me, that came from God, so I know it's right." Reverend Tom Gard smiled at Edmund. "The only thing you can do is pray and God will do what He has planned to do. Keep faith in your heart. Remember 'We live by faith, not by sight'. 2 Corinthians 5:7."

Edmund nodded. "I'll remember that one. Thanks for talking with me, Reverend."

Tom stood, walked around his desk, and shook hands with Edmund. "No problem. Any time you need to talk, I'm all ears."

Edmund took Kaitty home and waited for Tyler to come by and check her. He said he would be by every few days to see if there was any progress. He was sorry to say that there was no change.

"Ed, these things take time," Tyler said. "You just have to let it take its course. God will heal her when He wants, if He wants. Give Him time."

"I will. And I ask you to pray for her, if you can."

"I have been praying, for the both of you, every day. But it's God's Will, not ours, that will be done. Remember that."

A few days later, Edmund awoke to someone poking him on the arm. He rolled on his side, but he still felt the poking, this time on his shoulder.

"Edmund," someone said. He rolled over on his back again and opened his eyes. His vision was blurry. Rubbing his eyes, he saw Kaitty standing next to his bed, glowing with excitement.

"Kaitty," he said and he looked at the clock on the bedside table. "What are you doing up?"

"Edmund, I think I've gotten my memory back!"

Yeah, did you remember it's two in the morning? "How do you know?"

"I remember everything from my past. What my family was like, everything that's happened to me, even my birthday!"

"That's a start. I'll call Tyler in the morning and ask him to come over. But, until then, you need your sleep—and so do I."

"Sorry. I'll go back to bed." They kissed and she hurried off to bed.

The next morning, Edmund called his brother and asked him to come over there before he went to the hospital.

"Why? What's wrong?"

"Kaitty's gotten some of her memory back. I want you to see how much she's progressed."

When Tyler arrived, Kaitty was dressed and waiting on the couch for him. He went through the same procedure he did every time and raised his eye brows.

"She has gotten some memory back," he said. "In a couple of days she may regain all of her memory."

Edmund was glad. Once the memory loss was gone, they could focus on the wedding and prepare for their new life.

Chapter Three

Edmund was glad Kaitty got her memory back. Now they could focus on the wedding. They hadn't decided on anything yet. The first thing they wanted to do was to figure out when they were getting married. Each kept throwing out ideas on when, but they never agreed.

Edmund said, "Well, you don't want it to be late in the year, and I don't want it to be too early either, so sometime in the summer, right?"

"Yeah, but I still don't know when I think it would be best to have it."

"We'll think of something."

The time slipped by and before they knew it, it was April and they still hadn't decided on when to have the wedding. Kaitty needed to relax herself, so she decided that she would go to her favorite park. It always calmed her when she was with nature.

She watched as little children ran around, some trying to catch bugs. She watched people walking their dogs and some people sitting under trees. It was a sunny day and everything was blooming. She wished it could always be like this.

Then she saw, in the corner of her eye, that someone was watching her. A dark haired woman, no older than herself, was watching her from a picnic blanket under a tree with a man. The woman seemed more curious than suspicious. And, for some reason, she looked familiar to Kaitty.

Kaitty simply tried to ignore her, though she still felt the woman's eyes on her. She felt uneasy, so, following her instinct, she picked up her things and left for home.

As she was driving, she saw that she had three addressed envelopes that still needed to be sent off. She quickly drove to the post office and jogged inside. After she gave them to the postal clerk, she headed outside to her car.

She heard something. Footsteps. They came closer and closer from behind her. Kaitty turned around to see the same woman from the park walking up to her, the man that had sat next to the woman following in her wake.

Kaitty had to take action. She knew if they were to attack, it would be two against one and she would lose. She confronted the woman.

"Excuse me," she began, stopping and letting the two strangers walk up to her. "I would appreciate it if you didn't follow me."

The woman was a foot from Kaitty. Her brown eyes looked deeply into Kaitty's hazel ones. Then the woman said, "Kaitty?"

She was taken aback. How could a stranger know her name? "Who are you?" she asked.

"Anna Samuel...from boarding school. Don't you remember me?"

Kaitty was stunned. She could not even remember the last time she saw Anna. "Oh my gosh, how'd you find me?"

They hugged each other. When she was free, Anna answered, "I knew you had moved here when we finished high school. I didn't know if you still lived here, and it was a long shot coming here, but I guess I got lucky."

"Do you want to come back to my place?"

"Well, sure, but could—could my fiancé come, too?"

Kaitty looked, mouth agape, to the man standing behind Anna. "Well—uh—sure. But when we get home, we're both going to have a lot of stories to tell each other."

Kaitty pulled into the driveway of her home. Edmund's car sat out front, but he was nowhere to be seen. *He's probably wondering where I am.*

She got out of her car, and Anna and her fiancé, Jason Gilbert, followed Kaitty's lead. Together, they walked to the door; it was already unlocked. All three of them stepped in and found Edmund sitting at the kitchen table.

"Kaitty, where have you—who are they?"

"Edmund, this is my friend, Anna, from boarding school and this is her fiancé, Jason."

Edmund shook hands with both and asked, "Anna Samuel?"

"It will be Anna Gilbert soon," replied Anna.

"I haven't seen you since our high school years. You must tell us what you've been doing."

They all sat around the table and Anna told them about her life. "Once I got out of school, I started working at a hospital in Omaha as a nurse. I was still in college when I started working, so I was a nurse's assistant. Jason started working as a doctor there about a month before I did. We started getting together after work and decided we wanted to get married. So here we are. What about you two?"

Kaitty began. "I got out of school, never went home, except to get my things, moved here, got a job at the grocery store, now I'm engaged, and we'll be getting married soon."

"Still like you were during high school," joked Anna.

"What do you mean?" Kaitty asked.

"You always summed things up quickly. You never go into detail."

"Well, maybe I don't like details."

Anna laughed. "So, when's the wedding?"

"We haven't figured that part out yet," answered Edmund.

"What have you figured out?"

"Who we're marrying," He replied. They all laughed.

Kaitty enjoyed this. She hadn't seen her best friend in a long time, and here they were, sitting around the table, laughing at the stupid things they were saying.

She realized then how quickly her life was moving by. She had grown up, gone to school, and was preparing for a wedding, her wedding. She began to feel sad that everything seemed to go by in a hurry.

That night, Edmund could tell something was wrong with Kaitty. She had hardly touched her supper and they sat in silence. He was worried for her.

"Is something wrong, hon?"

Kaitty looked up from her untouched plate and stopped playing with her food. "I'm fine."

"Are you sure? Do you feel sick?"

"No, no—it's nothing—."

"So something is wrong! What is it, Kaitty?" He had stopped eating and placed a hand on hers.

"I told you, it's nothing—."

"It's not 'nothing' and you know it. Why won't you tell me?"

"Maybe because you don't need to know. I wish you were the same, quiet boy you used to be!"

She got up from her chair and ran upstairs. Edmund heard the bedroom door slam. He sat back in his chair and thought. What should he do? He had obviously set off some spark that made Kaitty go off. What if that happens again?

He prayed silently, *Lord, help us through this.*

He got up and walked upstairs. He stood outside Kaitty's door and listened to her sobs. He felt helpless, but something told him to go in there and sit with her. He went with this feeling.

She was lying in her bed, on her stomach, crying into her pillow. Edmund slowly made his way over to her and sat on the bed. He gently laid his hand on her shoulder and waited for her to look up. She finally did and pushed herself up into a sitting position. He looked into her red, puffy eyes. He had never seen her so upset.

"Tell me, what's wrong?"

Kaitty, sniffling, began to control herself then told him how she had been thinking about how fast her life seemed to be going. Edmund took her in his arms and held her close, gently rocking her. *So that's why she's upset,* he thought.

He let go of her and said, "Everyone has to grow up, and a lot of people look back and see their life and think it's going by too fast. But all you can really do is remember those things that you've gone through and live life to the fullest, 'cause, one day, you might not be here."

Kaitty smiled to her soon-to-be husband. He was right and that's what she was going to do from then on.

The next day, Kaitty and Edmund went to lunch with Anna and Jason. When the food was served, Kaitty asked if she could say the blessing. Anna had forgotten that Kaitty was a devoted Christian. She nodded, putting down her fork.

"Lord, we thank You for this food and for our friendship with each other. And we ask You that You would keep Anna and Jason safe while they visit here with us. Amen."

They began to eat. Kaitty wondered if Anna was a Christian, the same with Jason. She knew Anna had been once, but they had not spoken with each other for years. She was going to have to ask her about this when she had her alone next.

"Have you decided on a date for the wedding?" asked Anna.

Kaitty shook her head. "We can't think of a good time."

"Well, I thought of one last night," Anna continued. "How about August 9th?"

"August 9th? But that's my birthday."

"Exactly! What a better time? It's in the summer and it still gives you enough time to make all the arrangements and buy all the things you need."

"But why my birthday?"

Edmund put his arm around her and smiled. "What's a better present than getting married?"

It was decided then that they would marry on the 9th of August that year. Kaitty was nearly bursting with excitement. She wanted to start right away on the arrangements. Anna said that she would come along to help.

Were they back to being best friends?

Three months later

Kaitty and Edmund had decided on everything from the wedding gown to the cake they were having. They were both excited about it and could not wait to be married. It was two weeks before the wedding and they had to go in for the final fitting of her dress and his tux. Jason and Edmund had become closer and they, along with Tyler, went to get his tux. Kaitty, Anna, and Jana all went to get her dress.

Kaitty tried on her dress and the seamstress made sure it fit perfectly. She loved the dress and could not wait to walk down the aisle in it to the man of her dreams.

Edmund lead the way into the *Men's Tuxedo* store and asked for the suits under the name Lorenz.

"Uh, Sir, there's no suit listed for a 'Lorenz'," the woman at the counter said.

"I was in here three weeks ago. I had the suits ordered and they said they would be in by today."

"I'll check what we've ordered." And the woman hurried away.

Edmund turned to the other two and said in a quiet tone, "If they don't have them, somebody's gonna be in trouble!"

"Ed, it's alright," said Tyler. "Kaitty would understand that it wasn't your—."

"Not me! These people!"

The woman came back and said that there was nothing ordered for a "Lorenz" or "Carmichael" party. "The only person in here three weeks ago was an Edward Rolenc. Ordered a tux for himself and his groom's man; black, size 52 long for both."

"That's what ours were!" Edmund told her the address of his house and asked if that was "Edward Rolenc's" street. The woman was dumb-founded. Someone had made a mistake on the name when they put it in the computer. It so happened that the Edward Rolenc was really Edmund Lorenz.

Edmund and Tyler, despite the switching of the name, tried on their tuxes and headed home.

A week later

Kaitty and Anna sat at the kitchen table at Kaitty's house. They had had a long day and decided (along with Edmund, Tyler, and Jason) that this would be a perfect time to have the bachelor and bachelorette parties. The guys were out having theirs while Kaitty and Anna waited for Jana to arrive for the party.

"This really is a nice place," said Anna.

"Thanks," Kaitty replied. "What about yours? How nice is it?"

"It's really beautiful. Jason wanted this big house out in the country so bad that I had to give in for him."

"He lives with you?"

She nodded. "Is there something wrong with that?"

"Well, it kinda depends. Do you sleep together or in different rooms?"

"Together. Why, is that a prob—Oh, I forgot. You're a Christian."

"And I thought you were, too. In God's eyes—."

"I know, 'in God's eyes it would be like adultery.' I'm not stupid. You sound like my parents."

"That's because we care about you and your soul. 1 Corinthians 6:18-20 says, 'Flee from sexual immorality. All other sins a man commits are outside his body, but he who sins sexually sins against his own body. Do you not know that your body is a temple of the Holy Spirit, who is in you, whom you have received from God? You are not your own; you were bought at a price. Therefore honor God with your body.'"

"Why do we have to talk about this?"

"Because I don't want you to go to hell, I want you to have Christ in your life."

Anna stood and asserted, "Look, I know I was more like that when we were at school, but times have changed—and so have I." She stormed out of the house.

Edmund went to Kaitty's house that night. He couldn't find her anywhere downstairs, so he went to the second floor. He headed straight for her room and found her kneeling beside her bed, praying.

He would hate to disturb her, so he waited for a minute. Finally, she looked up, facing the opposite direction of him, and wiped her face. She appeared to be done praying, so he gently knocked on the open door.

She turned to look at him. Her eyes were red and puffy and she had tears streaming down her cheeks. He slowly walked over to her and helped her sit on the bed.

"What's with the tears?" he asked.

She sniffled and answered, "Nothing, it's just Anna."

"What's happened?"

She hesitated. "She and Jason sleep together."

Edmund was at loss for words. Anna...sleeping with someone...when she's not married to them...it didn't sound like the kind of person Anna was. "Isn't she Christian?"

"Obviously not any more. She said 'times have changed and so have I'. I couldn't say anything 'cause she walked out then and I don't think I would've known what to say if I had the chance. I had already quoted 1 Corinthians to her—I didn't know what to do."

Edmund soon left being assured by Kaitty several times that she would be fine. He said he would be over in the morning and they said goodnight.

Anna awoke the next morning, feeling an arm pulling her in, and then a hug and kiss on the cheek. She opened her eyes and saw Jason lying next to her.

"'Morning, beautiful," he said.

She rolled toward him and onto her stomach. "'Morning," she mumbled.

"I'm going to make breakfast."

Anna lay motionless on the bed as Jason went down to cook breakfast. She thought of what Kaitty had said the day before. Her friend seemed so annoying now. She knew her parents would not care what she did, but the thought lingered that her friend might be right.

Why was she so obsessed over this? She was a grown woman. She could do whatever she wanted. She didn't have to have someone controlling her actions. She didn't need any "God" in her life.

Suddenly, her room spun a little. Wait, it was her head. She felt slightly dizzy. Then it was gone.

What was that about? she thought.

The next morning Kaitty was constantly praying for Anna and Jason. She asked God to show them the way to Him and to help her find the words to say to help them.

Edmund came over and together they prayed. Their hearts were in it full force. They cared so much about these two souls, more than any souls in a long time. It was almost noon by the time they stopped. They made lunch and sat at the table. But as she ate, Kaitty still thought of her friend. She hoped with all her heart that Anna would be saved.

Six days later

It was the day before the wedding and Kaitty was determined to break through to Anna no matter what it took. She felt God giving her courage to talk to her and the want-to to do so. She didn't know how she would do it, but she knew God would give her the words when they were needed.

After the rehearsals were over, Kaitty asked Anna to come to her place. She was reluctant at first, but agreed. Edmund would meet them when he was done talking.

Kaitty and Anna sat in the living room. "I know why you wanted to talk to me," sighed Anna.

"Well, that saves me some breath. But, Anna, won't you just hear me out?"

"Just like my parents."

"Anna, please."

She was silent for a moment then said, "Alright, I'm all ears."

"I know who you used to be, and I believe that same girl is still inside you, you've just refused to accept it. God wants to be in your life, wants you to love Him, but you have rejected Him. You've said that you don't want a crutch, but He is much more than that. He will save you from your sins, He can make peace in your life, and He can guide you in life, but only if you let Him."

"I'm a good person, why would I need Him to 'save me from my sins'?"

"By whose standards? Yours or God's?"

"What would it matter? I'm not perfect but at least I've never killed someone or stole something."

"God's standards are so high that, in hating someone, you have murdered. In lusting after someone, you have committed adultery in your heart. Have you ever hated someone?"

"Well, haven't we all?"

"Just answer."

"Yes."

"Have you ever wanted something, cared about something more than God? Maybe a singer, a guy you had a crush on, a house?"

"Sure."

"Remember when you always disobeyed your parents when we were getting ready to graduate? God says that you should be respectful of your parents and to obey them. We both know you've broken that Commandment.

"God says you cannot lie. You've done that, too. So what does all this make you?"

She shrugged. "Human."

"Anna, if one person kills another person, that would make them a murderer. So if you lied that would make you what?"

"A liar."

"If you steal something that makes you—?

"A thief."

Kaitty reached out to the coffee table and pulled out her Bible from a cubbyhole. She flipped it open to the 10 Commandments in Deuteronomy 5. "Read these." She pointed to verse 7-21 and Anna read through them. "How many do you think you've broken?"

Anna thought for a moment then answered, "Seven, I guess. Two, and five through ten. So what? Are you saying that I need forgiveness?"

"Everyone needs forgiveness. You've broken seven of His Commandments. I've heard if you break one, you break them all." She paused for a minute. "Are you willing to accept Christ into your life—for good?"

Anna was in tears. She nodded, tears streaming down her cheeks. "But—how do I ask?"

"Repeat after me…." She got down on her knees in front of Anna and held her hands in hers. Anna repeated what she said. "Lord, I know I have sinned, and I ask You to forgive me of my sins. I have done wrong, but I want You in my life. I accept You into my heart and as my savior."

Kaitty looked up into her new sister's eyes and smiled. They hugged and Kaitty felt the presence of God with them. At that very moment, everyone in heaven was rejoicing for the new saved soul that was now Christ's forever more.

Chapter Four

The wedding had finally come the next morning. Anna and Jana had spent the night at Kaitty's place and they had the bachelorette party after the rehearsals. They stayed up late the night before and almost didn't wake up on time in the morning.

They ate and headed out to the beauty salon to get their hair and makeup done. Afterward, they went to lunch before heading to the church. The girls helped Kaitty into her dress, got on their dresses, and headed up into the parlor. By that time, it was an hour before the wedding.

"You guys should probably go over to the other side of the church, into the High School room, and wait there," said Kaitty.

"Are you sure?" asked Jana. "I don't want you to be all alone in here."

"I'll be fine. Just get over there and be ready to go out. I'll have one of the guys get you when it's time."

Anna and Jana seemed reluctant to leave, but did. Honestly, Kaitty didn't like being alone, but she needed time to collect her thoughts. This day was the beginning of her and Edmund's new life together. So many things started filling her head. What would happen through today? What would life be like with Edmund? Would they be together forever? Would she always love him and he the same? Did she even deserve him at all?

Edmund walked past the south doors to the parlor, up the east stairs, and into the vestibule. It was time to go up to the platform and await his bride.

He had a nervous breakdown. "Dad, I don't think I can do this."

"Relax, son. Everything will be fine."

"How? Kaitty's father isn't even here! She'll be walking down the aisle alone!"

"I'm walking her down the aisle. Everything will be fine. Now, it's time to get up there."

Edmund turned and walked out the doors and up onto the platform. *This is it,* he thought. *These are the last minutes of my old life. Time to start a new chapter.* He smiled at his own lame thought.

The bridesmaids and groomsmen started to walk out, met in the center, and walked down together. To him, it symbolized the beginning of his and Kaitty's new life.

Kaitty opened the parlor door when she heard a knock. "Are you ready?" asked Cameron.

"I guess." She followed her father-in-law-to-be up the stairs to the east vestibule. "I wish I wasn't walking down there alone," she said, watching the maid of honor and best man walk down.

"You won't be. I feel like I am your father, and if you would, I would like to walk you down to my son."

She was touched by his love and kindness. She nodded, tears filling her eyes, and took his arm. They walked out once the ring bearer and flower girl had gone. When she saw Edmund, she wanted to cry. He looked so handsome in his suit, silver vest, and silver striped tie. His hair was still messy, but she didn't mind. She loved it the way it was.

Edmund's heart seemed to stop when Kaitty started walking down the aisle. She looked so gorgeous as she came toward him, escorted by his dad. Her dress had no train, but as she walked it appeared to flow behind her. Her hair was up in a curly, messy bun, for the first time Edmund had seen in a long while. He tried to think of the last time he'd seen it this way, but his focus was solely on his beautiful bride walking to him.

They reached the front and the pastor said, "Well, I would ask who gives this woman to be married, but I was told not to."

The guests gave a soft laugh. Kaitty stepped up to Edmund and smiled.

The pastor began. "We have come here today to join these two in holy matrimony." He said a few verses and continued on. He finally came to the vows.

"Do you, Edmund Gabriel Lorenz, take Kaitty Lillian Carmichael to be your lawful wedded wife?" he asked.

"I do," said Edmund, focusing everything on Kaitty. They smiled and, for the first time they had been engaged, Edmund started to cry. It started Kaitty up.

"The ring, please," continued the pastor. Edmund's cousin, Johnny, came up, took the rings that were in his hand, and gave them to the pastor. "The ring symbolizes the never-ending bond of marriage. It never stops." He handed one of the rings to Edmund. "Now, repeat after me," he said to him. While Edmund slowly slipped the ring on Kaitty's finger, he repeated the words.

"I, Edmund Gabriel Lorenz…take you, Kaitty Lillian Carmichael…to be my lawful wedded wife…to have and to hold…for better or for worse…for richer or for poorer…in sickness and in health…to love and to cherish…and I promise to be faithful to you…till death do us part."

Kaitty did the same, though her voice quivered through tears of happiness.

"You may now kiss your bride," finished the pastor.

To Kaitty, no one else existed in the world at that very moment. But, when Kaitty and Edmund kissed, she knew she heard the crowd cheering and applauding.

"I am proud to present to you Mr. and Mrs. Edmund Lorenz."

They drove around in a limo for half-an-hour, taking pictures, then headed to the reception. They lined up in the order that they walked into the church and waited to be announced. Jana and Jason were announced. They walked in and went all the way over to the other side and stood behind their seats at the head table. The maid of honor, Anna, and the best man, Tyler, were next. They did the same as Jana and Jason. Once they were at the table, Kaitty and Edmund were announced and walked in to see a huge crowd of people seated at round tables. They danced a little as they made their way to the head table. They all sat once Kaitty and Edmund arrived at their seats. The announcer/DJ announced that the wedding party would get their food first at the buffet, followed by the immediate family, then one table at a time until everyone was served.

All of the wedding party served themselves and sat at the table again. Slowly everyone in the room made it up to the buffet once or twice. About an hour after the wedding party ate, they went over, stood behind the cake, and prepared to cut it. Tyler stood by Edmund and Anna by Kaitty. Tyler gave his speech and then Anna gave hers. Kaitty and Edmund cut the cake. They each took a piece and Edmund held his up to Kaitty's mouth; she took a bite and did the same with hers. Once Edmund took a bite, Kaitty took one of her fingers that had frosting on it and wiped it on Edmund's nose. The people started laughing. Edmund took his finger and did the same to Kaitty, wiping it on her nose.

Cameras flashed as people laughed and took pictures. Once Kaitty and Edmund stopped laughing, they took napkins and wiped off their noses.

The night progressed on with talking, laughing, and dancing. By midnight, Kaitty and Edmund finally went to their hotel room. When they stepped in, rose petals laid on the floor, the bed, and all around the room. Pictures that had been on the tables at the reception were placed on the TV stand, the dresser, and the bed-side tables.

They finally fell asleep. And the next day they began packing for their honeymoon. They would be leaving the next day for Hawaii. When that day came, they piled the bags in the back of the car and drove to the airport in Omaha. They checked in their bags and headed up the escalator to Terminal A on the right side of the airport. They went through security, bought some snacks, and sat down at Gate 3 to await their plane.

It arrived ten minutes later at 9 A.M., as scheduled, and they waited ten more minutes to board. They were last to board, but it didn't take long to get to their first class seats. They flew to Phoenix, Arizona and had a two hour layover.

They started walking down towards their gate and stopped at a restaurant for lunch. The second hour slowly passed, especially when they found out that all the seats were filled in the gate.

They stood for the longest time until this little boy, no older than eight, stood and offered his seat. Kaitty and Edmund politely declined and said for him to keep it. The boy kept trying, but he finally saw that they would not take his seat.

At that moment, the announcer said that the plane had landed and that they would be loading in a few minutes.

Kaitty tried to sleep on the second flight, but she couldn't. Eight hours on a plane did not sound good anymore. Edmund sat in the middle seat sound asleep and when Kaitty stared out the window, all that could be seen was water. She relaxed in her seat and tried again to fall asleep, this time with success.

She began to stir from her nap when she heard Edmund talking.

"You got a wife and kids?" Edmund asked.

The man replied, "We're expecting our first next month."

"Well congratulations! We just married the ninth."

"So you're honeymooners? Well congrats yourself! Where're you from?"

"Iowa. You?"

"Omaha, Nebraska. What part of Iowa?"

"Your side. I guess we're in the same neck of the woods."

Kaitty opened her eyes. Edmund had his arm around her, holding her close.

"'Morning, beautiful," he said.

"How long was I asleep?"

"'Bout an hour I think."

"I never expected it to be this long."

Edmund and the man sitting next to him chuckled. Edmund and said, "You can't expect eight hours to fly by, hon."

At around nine that night, they landed on the Big Island of Hawaii. By the time they had gathered their bags under a huge grass-looking hut at baggage claim, got in a bus that took them to a car rental place, got their car, and found their hotel, it was about half-after eleven. They sat on their bed in the suite and phoned room service. Once they ate, they turned on the TV and snuggled together in bed. Within thirty minutes, they were asleep.

The next morning they drove a few hours out to their second hotel. They checked in, dropped off their bags, and headed to look at the waterfalls nearby.

The water dropped off the rock and into a calmer pool of water. Kaitty couldn't think of a time that she had seen something as beautiful. The way the water flowed, the dazzling sound it made, everything. They made their way down a narrow path, avoiding others as they went, to the bank of the river. They took some pictures, asked someone to take their picture with the waterfall behind them, and then they made their way back to the hotel.

Their week there was long but pleasant. Kaitty was especially glad she didn't have to worry about the wedding anymore. And while they were there, Kaitty and Edmund found out that a couple from their church was there in Hawaii as well. They had lunch together and said their good-byes, then went on their way.

Kaitty was dreading the eight hour plane ride back to Phoenix, but she did miss her home and could not wait to move into their new house. Life was good for them, God was the center of their lives, and they were excited to start building a new life together.

Chapter Five

Three-and-a-half months had passed by since the wedding when Kaitty found herself sitting on the couch in her and Edmund's home on a cold November night, drowned in fear of telling her husband the news. Anna sat by her side, trying to ease her nerves.

"Well, when are you going to tell him?" asked Anna.

"I'm hoping when he gets home," she answered.

"You're hoping? What would happen?"

"I could lose my nerve."

"Well, when does he usually get home?"

"Normally at nine." She looked over at the wall clock.

"You alright?"

Kaitty looked to Anna and nodded, though she was not. "I'm just worried about how he'll take it. What if he doesn't want this right now? I mean, we just got married three months ago!"

"Kaitty, don't think that for one minute. He'll be very happy! Trust me. And why wouldn't he be home by now? It's almost eleven."

"I don't know. Something might have kept him at work."

Anna seemed excited, but Kaitty sat there in frightfulness. In the midst of her thoughts, she heard a car door open then slam shut. "He's here."

The door flew open to reveal Edmund. He slammed the door shut without looking at them. Kaitty could feel that he was already in a bad mood.

"Great day at work today," he said. "We found that one of our own soldiers is a spy, and now I have to clean up the mess."

"Edmund—," Kaitty tried, but he continued his ranting rage.

"I have to help change our codes and passwords so they can't get in and I have to finish it by tomorrow morning! I'm going to be up all night!"

He started for a door that led off of the living room to his office. Kaitty was determined to tell him her news right then no matter what it took.

"I'm pregnant."

"Fine, whatever," he said, without looking at her. Then he stormed into his office, slamming the door.

Anna held one of Kaitty's hands in her own and she tried to comfort her. But, not even five seconds after he stomped into his office, Edmund opened the door again and Kaitty looked up to him. He didn't look angry anymore. He looked dumb-struck.

He slowly walked into the living room, stood in front of Kaitty, took her hands, and pulled her onto her feet.

"Did you say you were—pregnant?"

She took a breath and, a little worriedly, said, "Yes."

He stared at her for the longest of time, and then shouted, "Kaitty! This is unreal! This is—this is—this is the best day ever!"

He pulled her into a tight embrace and gave her a long kiss.

Edmund finally let go and asked, "When did you find out?"

"Just this afternoon. Anna was here with me earlier when I started feeling weird. She became worried, took me along with to her checkup, and had the doctor check me out. The doctor came back and concluded that I was pregnant."

"Well, what are we waiting for? Let's tell my parents! Or have you already told them?"

"Ed, how are we going to tell them? They live forty-five minutes away, and I don't think they would appreciate a call this late. They're having Thanksgiving at their house tomorrow. Why don't we just tell them then?"

"Alright." He looked at Anna. "Anna, what're you doing here? It's past eleven."

"I phoned Jason and told him I might be late because I wanted to be with Kaitty until you got back," she answered. "But, now that you're here, I guess I'll just see you in the morning."

"Is Jason coming to church Sunday?"

"I'm afraid not, unless he changes his mind by then. I don't know what to do with him."

"We'll always be here for you if you need us," said Kaitty.

Anna had moved with them as they talked, and they now stood at the door. Anna put on her coat. She said a last good-bye and headed out the door.

After shutting the door, Edmund turned around to face his wife. He pulled her into a hug and kissed her on the head. "My beautiful wife…"

"My tall husband…"

He laughed. "I'm serious, honey. God led me to you and now He has blessed us with a baby." He kissed her. "What more could a man want?"

The next morning, Kaitty and Edmund woke around nine, and packed their things into the car. They drove over to Anna and Jason's to pick them up, then headed up to Kaitty's in-laws' house in Council Bluffs.

About forty-five minutes later, they arrived at the house and began unloading all the things in the back. Cameron and Christine came out to help them.

"Oh, it's so nice to see you two," said Christine when they finished unloading.

"It's nice to see you, too," said Kaitty, hugging her.

Kaitty and Edmund sat around talking to everyone while the food finished cooking and the table was set. Kaitty was able to pull Tyler away from everyone else for a moment.

"You didn't tell them, right?"

"No. I was sure you would want to tell everyone after you told Edmund."

"Well, I thank you for that."

"It's no problem. But I can't believe I'm going to be an uncle!"

"Shh! Keep it down! I don't want them to know yet."

He laughed a little. "Sorry."

Once the table was set, everyone was seated. Cameron said the blessing and, before anyone could start eating, Edmund stood and said he had an announcement to make. "As you all know, Kaitty and I have been married about three-and-a-half months. Well, just last night, we found out that we are awaiting a new little blessing. Kaitty's pregnant!"

All at once, everyone was saying, "Congratulations," and, "That's wonderful!"

"When are we expecting this new arrival?" asked Cameron.

"The beginning of August," Kaitty answered.

"That's great!" Jana chimed in.

"Not to be pushy," said Tyler, "but can we eat now?"

"Yes, dig in everyone!" said Cameron.

Everyone enjoyed their time together. Before they went home, Kaitty and Edmund made plans to spend the next day with his parents. They loaded the car again and started the near hour drive home.

That night, Edmund came from the upstairs bathroom into their bedroom to find Kaitty lying under the covers, reading her Bible. He crawled into bed next to her, snuggled in close, and wrapped his arm around her.

"You know, I think this is the first time since this morning that I've had you to myself," he said.

"Well, maybe that's because you don't know how to sneak me away from crowds."

He chuckled and kissed her on the cheek. "I love you, babe."

"I love you, too."

They kissed. "Now, it's getting late. Let's get some sleep."

They slept in that morning. Once they woke, they spent an hour sitting around and then headed to Edmund's parents'.

When they first arrived, they talked with them for a couple of hours after eating lunch. They sat down at the table again around seven-thirty and ate dinner. As they were finishing dessert, someone knocked on the door. Christine answered it and came back with a frantic Jason. Kaitty started to say something, but Jason answered her before she could speak.

"Anna's in the hospital. The doctors don't know what it is yet, but she was having terrible stomach pains."

"Slow down, Jay," said Kaitty. "Now, what happened?"

Jason spilled the story. "We were visiting my family out in Omaha. About an hour ago I took her to the ER 'cause she was having stomach pains that were starting to worsen, and she was bleeding, too. I left her at the hospital with my parents to come here, and I really want to get back to her."

They gathered their coats and headed out of the house. They arrived about fifteen minutes later at the hospital and hurried to the front desk to find what room Anna had been placed in. They piled into an elevator and started to go to the third floor. They found Anna in room 320 along with Jason's parents.

"How're you doing, sweetie?" he asked as he bent over to kiss her on the forehead.

She began to cry. "The doctors said that I've had a miscarriage. Jason, I'm sorry...."

He clearly had a lump in his throat. "It's not your fault, honey. These things—they just happen."

Tyler walked into the room, hands in the pockets of his white lab coat. "Tyler," said Jason, "is there anything—?"

He shook his head. "I'm sorry. I wish there were, but there isn't."

"Will Anna be alright though?"

"I'm certain she will, but I want to keep her here a few days and monitor her. She should be going home Sunday evening if everything goes well. I'll be back around in about an hour."

Tyler walked out of the room. Kaitty took a spot beside the bed and hugged Anna. "Things will be alright," she said.

"Kaitty, why do these things happen?" Anna asked. "Couldn't God have prevented it?"

"I think he could, but maybe He wants it was to happen for something else to come from it, something good."

"Why would this have happened to me? Why not to you?"

She was shocked at her last question. She knew Anna didn't mean it. "I don't know, Anna. I believe all things happen for a reason. I also believe that God lets certain things occur for something good to happen and to make us stronger."

"What good would come out of losing a baby?"

"I don't know. God has planned out what will happen. All you need to do is walk by faith, not by sight. Trust in Him."

"How? I'm new to all of this, you know."

"Well, if God decided something should happen, in your life or another's, then you should embrace that decision."

She paused. "Where's Jason? He was here a second ago."

"I'll go find him." She got up from her chair and stepped out of the room. There he sat to her left, face buried in his hands. She heard muffled wails come through from the buried face.

Kaitty walked over to him, put a hand on his shoulder, and knelt beside him. He didn't move or speak. He just sat there, mourning.

"Jay," she said gently.

"It's my fault," he said. "It's my fault she's in here."

"Jay, it's not your fault."

"Yes it is!" He looked up from his hands. "If I hadn't gotten her pregnant, then she wouldn't be in here. It's my fault!"

He began to sob again, but he didn't cover his face. He slid off the chair and knelt on the floor like Kaitty. She took him by the shoulders and pulled him to her and hugged him. Jason grasped his arms around her and shook as he sobbed into her shoulder.

Kaitty closed her eyes and began to pray.

Chapter Six

Kaitty pulled away from Jason, who stared at the ground, wiping tears away from his face. She helped him to his feet, sat him in a chair, and plopped into the one next to him.

"Jason, Kaitty!" came a frantic voice. Kaitty looked up to see Mr. and Mrs. Samuel running to them. "Where is she? Where's our daughter?"

"She's in there," Kaitty answered, pointing to the room. "But I must warn you, she's very upset."

Anna's parents stepped into the room. Kaitty put a hand on Jason's shoulder.

"Jay, it's not your fault. These things can just happen. You can't change the past. If you didn't marry Anna, both of you would probably be just as unhappy. God has planned what will happen for you two."

"God? If there is a God, then He certainly isn't interested in me or Anna, or else our baby would still be alive! You and Anna always say 'God is good'. Well, how? How is He good when He takes away our child? Tell me, how?"

"When things like this happen, it's not God's doing. But all things happen for a reason, Jay."

"What? Is He saying that we wouldn't be good parents if we had a child, so He took him away?"

Kaitty did not want to argue with him. She understood that he was in a lot of pain over the loss of their unborn child, but she could not help trying to get him to Christ. Oh, how she knew he needed Christ in his life!

Tyler came down the hall and asked Kaitty to come with him to his office. She followed him and, once in the room, Tyler leaned up against his desk, tired and concerned.

"Kaitty," he said softly, "I think the baby is gone. Anna will be fine and will be able to have more kids, but I think it's too late for this one."

Kaitty looked up, tears in her eyes. She gave a slight nod and looked down. "I think you should've told them first."

"I didn't know how they would take it. Since you're a believer in Christ and know them better, I was hoping that you would be able to help them."

"How?"

"Take Jason to the church services on Sunday. Show him that there is a loving God looking after them. Tell him that there is a heaven and there is a hell. Tell him that their unborn child is up in heaven with Him, happy to be there. He may come around after a while. I know Anna's a believer."

"How long?"

"Only God knows, and only they can decide. We just have to keep praying. You know what you need to say. You don't have to plan anything, just tell them the answers they need to hear, before or after they ask. You know—the works."

"It's not as easy as it seems, though."

"I know." He stood up and held out a hand to her. She took it. "Let's go tell them."

They walked back to the room where the others still waited. "Tyler, what's happened to our daughter?" asked Mrs. Samuel.

Kaitty looked to Tyler. He nodded and Kaitty said, "She's all right, but—." She stopped and looked up to Tyler again.

"But it's too late to save the baby," he finished, slowly.

Mrs. Samuel gave way to tears as her husband held her. "Will she be able—?" started Mr. Samuel. Tyler nodded. Mr. Samuel sighed. "How long will she be in here?"

"We want to keep her here a few days for observation. She should be going home Sunday afternoon if everything goes well."

That night, Kaitty and Edmund took Jason home. They worried for him. He never spoke a word except to tell them thanks for the ride.

Kaitty crawled into bed next to Edmund and kissed him on the cheek.

He set down his Bible and looked to her. "What was that for?"

"Just for nothing. I love you."

"Love you, too, babe." They kissed again and went to bed.

———————

Edmund awoke early the next morning and cooked breakfast for him and Kaitty. She woke to the smell of hot, cooking pancakes.

She slowly tossed the covers from her, slipped her robe on over her pajamas, and walked barefooted downstairs. She strolled into the kitchen to find Edmund standing over the stove, flipping pancakes.

She snuck up behind him and wrapped her arms around him. He covered her hands with one of his.

"I thought I heard a mouse," he said. "Do you want to put the syrup in the microwave? The pancakes will be done in a second."

She did and once the food was done, they sat at the table, said the blessing, and served themselves.

After eating, Kaitty and Edmund said good-bye and planned to meet at the hospital after he got done with work. They kissed, hugged, and exchanged "I love you" to each other.

Once he left, Kaitty trudged upstairs and changed. After that, she began to look around the room. *What a pig's sty,* she thought. She made the bed and commenced the cleaning process. Why did she never clean until it was in extreme muddle?

She cleaned and swept and organized until she received a call from Anna.

"You feeling better?" she asked as she settled into the couch, cell phone to her ear.

"Physically, yeah, mentally, no."

"Oh, it'll be alright, Anna. God will give you another child, I'm positive. Ed and I'll be up there again tonight after his shift. Is Jason with you?"

"Yes. He's been here since about nine." There was an awkward silence. Then, "Kaitty, can I tell you something?"

"Of course, you know you can."

"Well, I feel like I've hurt Jay. I mean, I was the one who was supposed to care for the baby, and I've let them both down."

"Anna, it's not your fault. These things just happen. You couldn't have done anything to help."

"But why did it have to be me? Why'd it have to happen to *my* baby?"

"Well, maybe God's using this to reach out to Jay. Maybe this was meant to get him to change and become saved, to reach out for God's hand and to have Him lead the way out of his pain."

"Well *that* hasn't happened yet. At least twice I've heard him curse to God for letting our baby die."

"Well, it's not going to happen simultaneously. It'll take time with him."

The call ended shortly after and Kaitty resumed cleaning. She finally finished half-an-hour before she had to head to the hospital. So she sat down on the couch and gazed at the channels, looking for something to watch.

The half-hour had rolled by and she soon found herself in the car headed to Council Bluffs.

She arrived at the hospital early and headed up to Anna's room. When she walked in, Anna was playing a round of Kings Corners with Jason.

"There's really nothing to do here, you know."

Kaitty chuckled and pulled a chair up to the bed.

"Where's Ed?" Jason asked.

"Still at work. I'm early anyway. You doing okay, Jay?"

"Better than I was."

"Bored just sitting here?"

"No worse than usual."

"Well, I beg to differ!" Anna protested.

"I was just about to say that," Kaitty said. "I could never be put in here for more than an hour. I'd go mad. No privacy at all."

"You're telling me."

Edmund arrived a little later and they visited for awhile. Kaitty had a chance of talking to Jason alone and took it for what she could.

"Jay, I want to talk to you."

"Okay. Should I be sitting down?"

She ignored his comment. "With what's happened, I really think you should come to church with us tomorrow."

"What, because I need to 'get religious'? First Anna, now you? I don't believe in this crap. It may work for others, but I don't need and/or want a crutch through life!"

"Jason, please! Do it for Anna. Don't you think she would want you to do this? Wouldn't you do it for her, to give her something to be joyful about?"

"Joyful about what?"

"Knowing that you're one step closer to where we all want you to be! Look at her." Jason looked and observed his beautiful wife, struggling to show a smile. "Do you want her in more pain of knowing that, if you die, where you're going right now is not the place she can meet you again when you're both gone? Do you want her to feel that she's let you down again? It's not her or my decision whether you choose to accept God or continue to cast Him away. We can only tell you what we know and what His message is to you. He loves you and wants you to be with Him for eternity."

They stood there for a moment, neither moving nor talking. After a few moments, Jason stepped back into the room. Kaitty looked around the hall. Some people were staring at her. She ignored them and sat down in a vacant seat. She bowed her head and began to pray.

Lord, please help them through this hard time. Do whatever it takes to help them, even if You use me. I know You have great power and I just ask that you would help Jason to see the truth. I will do all that I can to show him the way to You. Amen.

Someone touched her shoulder. She lifted her head to find Tyler kneeling beside her. "Are you alright?"

She nodded. "Just asking God for help. Hopefully Jason will come with us."

"Trying to get him to go to church? Well, I hope you made a convincing argument."

"I don't know. I just hope I'm not pushing him away. That's the *last* thing I want to do."

"Well, you just have to be patient."

"*That's* a problem and we all know it! I'm not the patient type."

"God knows what will happen and when. If He planned him to go, then he will."

A minute or so before Kaitty and Edmund were to leave, Jason pulled Kaitty aside and spoke with her. "I talked with Anna and I've decided that—I'll go."

She told him that they would pick him up at nine the next morning for church. He said he would be ready.

The next morning, Kaitty and Edmund picked Jason up a little after nine and headed to the First Presbyterian Church. When they arrived, Kaitty pulled Edmund aside when he stepped out of the car. "Could you take Jay to our pew and keep him there while I go talk to the pastor?"

He nodded. "What if this doesn't work, Kaitty?"

"Have faith in the Lord, Ed. He'll help him. Don't doubt."

Edmund did as instructed and took Jason to their pew while Kaitty looked for the pastor.

She began to search for the pastor. She walked through the church office and into the pastor's connecting office to find him sitting at his desk, reading over his notes

"Kaitty!" he said. "It's good to see you! How have you and Edmund been?"

"Well, I've been fine," answered Kaitty. "I just found out this week that Ed and I—are expecting."

He cocked his head and unfolded his hands. "Expecting what?"

"Well, you know," said Kaitty. He looked confused. "When two people get married—."

"You're pregnant," cut in the pastor. "You've only been married for, what, three months? Well, congratulations!"

"Thank you, but that's not why I came to talk to you, Tom."

"Then what is it?"

Kaitty began to pace around the small office. "Well, you know my friends Jason and Anna Gilbert, right?" Tom nodded. "Well, Anna was four months pregnant."

"Was?" asked Tom.

"Well, my brother-in-law, Tyler, says that she had a miscarriage. Anna's already a follower of Christ, and I wanted to bring Jason to Christ, too."

"Well, that's a very good idea, Kaitty. Has he ever been exposed to this type of thing before?"

"I don't know. I've only known him for a few months and I still don't know much about his past. The only times I know of is when Anna, Ed, and I talk to him about it."

"We're probably going to have to start out slow then. We don't want to push him to the breaking point on the first week."

"I'll try not to, but you know me. I'm a very outspoken person. It's hard to keep these things from coming out—harshly."

"I know what you mean. But it's something God wants us to control. We can at least try our best."

"I will, don't worry. Oh, and please don't announce that Ed and I are going to be parents. He wanted to publicize it. I don't want to ruin it for him."

"I promise."

Kaitty went back out to Edmund and Jason, who sat in the fifth pew from the front on the right hand side. She sat down next to Edmund by the aisle and whispered in his ear, "I talked to Tom and told him everything. He thinks it's a good idea."

He gave a slight nod and looked back up to the pulpit as Tom came up to the stand.

"Welcome, everyone," he said. "Now, I know we have a newcomer here with us today by the name of Jason Gilbert." He looked to Jason on the other side of Edmund and smiled. "Since I have also heard that you have never come here before, I would just like to introduce myself. My name is Tom Gard and I am the pastor here. We all welcome you today, Mr. Gilbert. Now, the announcements for today—I would just like to say that Mr. Gilbert was brought here today by Kaitty and Edmund because something terrible has happen to him and his wife.

"He has been married for about three months now and his wife was four months pregnant with their first child. But on Friday, the doctor everyone here knows as Tyler Lorenz concluded that Mrs. Anna Gilbert had a miscarriage and I believe they could use some special prayers.

"Is there any other announcements of joy or sorrow that would like to be shared?"

Edmund quickly raised his hand and Tom called upon him. "Yes, Edmund?"

Edmund stood and began. "Well, despite what happen with our friends, Kaitty and I have found out that we are going to be parents." All around there came applause and cheers.

"When is this new member of the church's family expected?" asked Tom.

"August 7th."

"We wish you Godspeed with this new blessing." Tom stopped for a moment, looked down and then back up and continued. "Children are a blessing from God. Let us be wise to know this and good to cherish it. Now, if you will open up your hymnal to hymn number 343, Amazing Grace, and sing along with us in praise this morning."

Everyone stood and began to sing. Once the song was over, everyone sat back down. Tom began to tell the message.

"Two men dressed in pilots' uniforms walked up the aisle of the aircraft. Both were wearing dark glasses, one was using a guide dog, and the other tapped his way along the aisle with a cane. Nervous laughter spread through the cabin, but the men entered the cockpit, closed the door, and the engines started up. The passengers began glancing nervously around, searching for some kind of a sign that this is just a little practical joke.

"The plane moved faster and faster down the runway and the people sitting in the window seats realized they were headed straight for the water at the edge of the airport property. Just as it begins to look as though the plane will plow straight into the water, panicked screams filled the cabin.

"At that moment, the plane lifted smoothly into the air. The passengers relaxed and laughed a little sheepishly, and soon all retreated into their magazines and books, secure in the knowledge that the plane was in good hands. Meanwhile, in the cockpit, one of the blind pilots turned to the other and said, 'You know, Bob, one of these days, they're gonna scream too late and we're all gonna die!'

"Now that's something you wouldn't forget! Life is all about trusting in God, that He will hold us, take care of us, and comfort us whenever we need it. Let's bow our heads for prayer."

After church, Kaitty suggested that Jason go home and get some rest before it was time to pick up Anna. Jason, after some arguments, agreed.

He trudged up into his empty house, into his bedroom, changed, got in bed, and fell asleep.

There he sat in his living room, watching everyone enjoy themselves in chatter. In a flash, everyone was gone; he was all alone. He stood up, looked around, and started to search around the house for someone, anyone, who had been left with him. After searching everywhere (upstairs, downstairs, and outside), Jason came back to the living room, plopped down on the couch, and buried his face in his hands.

"Where are they?" he wondered aloud, and he began to shed tears. He realized that he was all alone with nobody to tell him what had happened. Then, a glorious bright light blinded him through his fingers and when he looked up, shielding his eyes, he saw a man dressed in a white robe, with Anna beside him, walking up to him.

"Do not fear," the figure said. "The people that you know and love are in Heaven with the Lord God, your Father and Creator. They are there waiting for you to join them. Accept Christ; bring Him into your life."

"Who are you?" Jason asked, his eyes finally adjusting to the light.

"I am the Angel Gabriel sent from God to give you the message that you need to accept Him so that you will have ever lasting life in heaven with your friends and family. God loves you, Jason, and He wants you to live with Him in His house when the end comes. Will you accept Him into your life as your Savior?" Jason was silent. The angel Gabriel finished by saying, "Y'shua hamashiach."

Jason woke with a scream. He was covered in cold sweat and panting. *What was that about*, he thought. *And what did that mean? What was it?*

"Y'shua hamashiach," he said aloud. "What does that mean?" He didn't know what to do. He looked at the clock; it read 11:05 A.M.. *Why did it only take two minutes? Would the pastor still be at the church?* He quickly got dressed, grabbed his keys, and drove to the church. He pulled up to the front of the church to see Tom Gard locking the door.

"Pastor!" he yelled, stepping out of the car.

Tom turned on the spot. "Hello, Mr. Gilbert," he said cheerfully. "What brings you back here?"

Jason jumped up the four steps and stood in front of Tom. "I needed to ask you something."

"Well, of course. Come in."

They walked into the sanctuary and Tom gestured to the pew closest to the front. Jason sat and stared fixedly ahead at the bottom of the stage in front of him. Tom sat next to him and sighed.

"Did you want to talk about what's happened?" asked Tom.

"No. That's not why I came." He sighed. "I needed to ask you something."

"I'm all ears."

"What does 'Y'shua hamashiach' mean?"

Tom looked astounded. "Where did you hear this from?"

Jason braced himself and began to recall the dream.

Tom was speechless. "Yes, I know what it means, and I'm surprised you had a dream like that. Y'shua hamashiach means 'Jesus the Messiah', Jason."

"Well, what was my dream about then?"

"Well, I think it was a message from God on the wings of the Angel Gabriel to tell you that you need to be saved."

"Why? Why would He send a message to me? I'm nothing important. Kaitty and Edmund are more of believers than I am. Why would God care about me? Pity me for my dead baby?"

"Son, God loves all His children, no matter what. Never forget that. He sent you the message because you need Him; you need Him in your life, in your relationships, in your heart. If you do not confess your sins to Him, you will go to hell. I believe that dream might've been a glimpse of the rapture, which means your family went to Heaven, but you were left behind on the earth that is going to become, literally, a living hell. If you have not become a true Christian, have not been faithful to God, or even have not confessed your sins, then you will be left behind if the rapture occurs within your life time. If you die before you've confessed your sins and ask to be forgiven, then you will go to hell."

"But if He loves me so much, then why did He let my baby die?" he shouted, standing up.

"Because God wanted that child home with Him. When something like that happens, it's because He planned it like so. And maybe it's for some kind of good to come from it."

"But why would I worship someone who let my baby die?"

"This is exactly what I'm talking about, Jason! You need to come to Christ, to become saved, not this route you're on! Please. Please, just think about it."

Jason thought on it for a moment, then said, "I'll think about it, but I'm not promising anything."

"And if it's all right, I wanted to go and visit your wife."

"I'll drive you there."

Jason drove himself and Tom to the hospital. Neither said a word along the way. When they arrived, Jason parked in the lot, got out, and waited for Tom to come around to the other side. They walked up to the hospital, still not saying anything. He led the way to Anna's room.

Anna was already awake when they came in. Kaitty was sitting on the farthest side of the bed.

"Jay," Anna said, holding out her hand to him. He stepped over, took her hand, bent over, and kissed her.

"I'm glad you went to church with Kaitty and Edmund. Oh, hello Tom. I suppose you've heard why I'm here."

"Unfortunately, yes."

"Anna, why don't you get some rest," Jason persuaded. "You'll be going home soon." She didn't say anything, just laid back into her pillow, closed her eyes, and drifted to sleep.

There were a few moments of silence. Then, "Kaitty, where's Edmund?"

"Bathroom. So, what are you doing here, Tom?"

Tom looked to Jason as if to get permission to speak. He gave a nod and Tom plunged into the story.

Jason held up a hand to stop him before he could tell of the dream. "I want to tell her," he said simply. Tom nodded and Jason picked up from where he left off. He retold the story of what happened again, telling of Gabriel and what the angel had said to him.

When he finished, Anna began to talk in her sleep. "Jesus the Messiah..." Jason looked up to Kaitty; she was startled. He looked over to Tom; his eyes were bulging and his mouth was open.

Anna started again, mumbling in her sleep. "Jason, please...come to Jesus...Be with us forever...I don't want to see you banished to pain and suffering...Be with me...."

No one knew what to think or say. "Gabriel has told you...Do you not love me?...Why do you not listen to him?"

"Tom—."

Tom stood, stepped over to Jason, knelt in front of him, and took his hands. "Pray with me," he said. They bowed their heads and he repeated after Tom. "Lord I know You are my savior, and I know I have sinned. Please forgive me of my sins. I invite You into my life from this point on and I ask that You will guide me through my life. Amen."

Jason lifted his head. He felt a kind of peace in him now. He knew Jesus was there with him. *Is this always how you feel?* he puzzled.

"Jay, what's up with all this?" Kaitty asked. She was almost speechless.

He looked to her. "I think I just accepted Christ into my life. How did you feel when you did it?"

Kaitty pondered for a moment. "Well, I guess I kinda felt—at peace. That's the only way to describe it."

He nodded though in shock; you really *couldn't* describe it any other way.

Someone knocked on the door. Tyler walked in and asked, "How is she today?"

"She's fine," said Kaitty. "She's been sleeping for a bit."

He walked up to Anna and took a quick glance over her. "I wouldn't let her sleep much longer. If she doesn't wake in an hour, wake her. She's been sleeping a lot. It wouldn't be good for her. I'll be back in half-an-hour."

He walked out of the room and continued on his rounds. Once he was gone, Anna slowly woke. "Jay?"

"I'm right here, honey," he said, leaning over and taking her hand. "What is it?"

"I had a dream," she answered. "It's strange. I couldn't understand it very well."

"What happened?"

"An angel appeared to me and told me that he had appeared to you, too. Then he kept on saying—Y'shua hama-...Y'shua—I can't remember—."

"Y'shua hamashiach."

Anna cocked her head. "Yeah. How did you..."

"I did have a dream where an angel appeared to me. He said 'Y'shua hamashiach' meaning 'Jesus the Messiah'. Hon, I'm now a follower of Christ. I heard you saying 'Jesus the Messiah' in your sleep. Then you started saying things like—.

"'Do you not love me?' and 'Why do you not listen to him?'?"

He nodded. "I knew I needed Him."

She sat up and embraced him. "I'm glad you've come around."

She quickly let go of him and put a hand on her stomach. "Jay—." She took one of his hands and put it next to hers. There was a gentle beat. His feet seemed to have a mind of their own as he ran from the room to find Tyler. He returned moments later, Tyler galloping at his side.

"I swear I felt something!" Tyler sighed and began to examine Anna. He stopped. There it was, just as Jason had described, a soft beat coming from Anna's stomach.

Tyler called for a nurse to get an ultra-sound machine in there immediately. He set the machine up and began looking at the screen as it showed the inside of Anna's stomach. His eyes began to pop when he'd seen two legs kicking slightly and heard the *thud-thud, thud-thud* sound of the little baby's heart. He let out a laugh.

"I don't believe it!" he said. "This baby was gone! I know it was! All I know is that you two are going to be parents!"

There were cheers and laughter.

Later on that night, when Anna was home, Jason, Anna, Kaitty, Edmund, and Tyler all silently prayed together thanking God for the second chance and for the new soon-to-be newborn child.

Jason knew that there was someone looking out for his family and was glad to be a part of God's family.

Four months later

Anna sat in the living room of her and Jason's home. It was ten in the morning and Jason had left for work two hours previous. Being near due, the hospital released her on maternity leave.

She was glad to be able to rest on the couch without having to do anything. Although she had to admit that it was boring after some time. There just weren't enough channels to watch or books to read.

She felt cramping. *Please, Lord,* she prayed silently. *Don't let this be bad.*

She went into the bathroom and tried to use the toilet, but nothing was coming. Then a searing pain struck her. She tried not to scream, but she let out a long grunt.

The baby's coming.

She trudged out of the bathroom. She grabbed her phone from the couch and called Jason.

"Hey, honey. I'm working on a patient."

"Well, you have another one. The baby's coming."

"*What?* How far apart are the contractions?"

"About every fifteen minutes."

"Alright, listen, babe. I want you to call Kaitty or Edmund and have them bring you up here. I'll set up a room for you for when you get here. Until they arrive there to pick you up, I want you to relax, okay?"

"Alright. I'll see you in a bit."

They hung up.

Another doctor came up to Jason.

"Hey, your patient's asking for you." Jason turned around to look at him with astonishment. "Hey, you alright?"

"I'm having a baby."

"What?"

"Anna, she just called me. I'm having a baby!"

"Congrats!"

"Thanks. I need a room to be set up for her. She'll be up here in about an hour-and-a-half."

"Alright, I'll get going on that. You want me to take care of your patient too?"

"No, I'm heading there now. Let me know when my wife is here."

As Anna waited for Kaitty to arrive, she tried her best to relax. Her bag was packed and she was ready to have this baby. She could not wait to hold that little newborn in her arms.

Then she was scared. What if something happened during or after he was born? What if she could not teach her son right? It would be all on her head for how their little Anthony turned out.

Kaitty came in the door. "You ready?"

"As I'll ever be, I guess."

"Come on, I'll grab your bag and we'll head up there. Edmund will meet us there."

Kaitty quickly tossed Anna's bag into the car and came back to help her. She raced up to Omaha, signals flashing. "Nervous?" she asked Anna.

"No more than usual."

"Everything will be alright. We'll all be by your side. Nothing's going to happen."

Anna smiled. She loved how Kaitty was always so heartfelt. It lifted her spirits about this whole thing.

Seven hours later

After eight hours of labor, Anthony Samuel Gilbert was born. A beautiful baby boy who weighed 7 pounds, 8 ounces. Anna and Jason were so happy. Their own little blessing was now in their arms.

Chapter Seven

Eight months later...

Edmund slowly stirred the pot of noodles. He snatched a few seasonings and added them to the pot.

"Kaitty!" he called. "Are you almost done?"

"Just a minute!"

"Well, you'd better hurry!" *I think I'm starting to burn the food.*

"Just stir the noodles—and don't add anything to it!"

"I won't!" He franticly took the spoon and tried to get the seasonings out.

"Hum—." He turned to see Kaitty standing in the doorway. Her belly was clearly defined under her green silk blouse, proving she was very pregnant.

"Does this top make me look fat?"

He chuckled. "Why do I feel that there's no right answer to that? You do know you're eight months pregnant, right?"

"Honestly, how do I look?"

He walked to her and held her by the shoulders. "Like you're married to the luckiest man on this earth." They kissed. Edmund drew back and looked into Kaitty's eyes. "What's wrong?"

"Nothing, it's just—well, I've never met your uncle before. What if he doesn't like me?"

He smiled and chuckled. "Kaitty, relax! It's just my Uncle Hedrick! He'll love you, trust me."

The doorbell rang. "I'll get it," he said. He walked to the door, straightened his shirt, and invited them in.

"Edmund, boy!" someone said. "I haven't seen you since you were ten!"

"Nice to see you, too, Uncle Hedrick," said Edmund simply. "Hi, mom, dad."

Christine stepped in and kissed Edmund on the cheek. "I can't believe how fast you grew up."

"Mom," he whispered. "I'm an adult and married!"

She shook her head. "You'll always be my little boy."

Her mind was at war with itself:
Go greet them.
No. You don't want to look too eager.
But you need to be polite. Now go!
No, stay! Wait for Ed to call you in!
Ugh!

Eventually, Kaitty made up her mind and walked out to the group. Edmund lured her in with an open arm. "Uncle Hedrick, I'd like you to meet my beautiful wife, Kaitty."

Hedrick took one look at her and his eyes widened. "She's pregnant?" he asked.

"Well, don't sound so surprised, Hedrick," said Cameron. "They truly love each other."

"But they were just married."

"Um, that was almost a year ago, Uncle Hedrick," Edmund reminded. "Anyway, come in and have a seat over in the dining room. Supper's almost done."

Once Edmund had closed the door, Kaitty leaned over and whispered, "It's that noticeable?"

He chuckled. "Eight months, remember?" *I hope this self-consciousness leaves when the baby's born.*

"Well, I'm really sorry I missed the wedding," Hedrick was saying. "Sounds like you had a good time."

"Yeah," replied Edmund. "Why couldn't you come, though?"

"Mmm, business trip."

"You got a job now?" Cameron asked.

Hedrick nodded. "A—uh—police officer. Sorry, lost my train of thought."

"Well, that's a good job to take up," said Kaitty.

He seemed to ignore her. She looked down at her plate, shutting her mouth. Was this the hormones working at her?

"When will you be heading back to Chicago?" Edmund asked.

"Oh, right after I finish some business here."

"Won't you be missing your family, being so far from them so long?" Kaitty asked.

He froze. He looked troubled at the mention of his family. Then he began to look enraged. "I think it's time I leave."

"You won't be able to get into the house." Christine said.

"I have a room in a hotel reserved. I'll see you later. Good-bye."

He quickly threw on his coat and strode out the door, slamming it behind him.

They all looked down at the table. "Honey, I think it's time we go. We may be able to catch him," said Cameron.

"I'll walk you out," Edmund volunteered.

Edmund closed the front door behind him as he stood with his parents out on the porch. "I should've reminded Kaitty not to say anything."

"Oh, Ed, it's not your fault. Anyone could have made that mistake."

"Mom, she doesn't remember. Therefore it was my fault for her 'mistake'."

"Edmund, it'll be alright," said Cameron. "We'd better go and try to find Hedrick. We shouldn't leave him alone in this state."

"Why?"

He sighed. "He had, one time, tried to—kill himself."

Edmund's mouth dropped. "Uncle Hedrick tried to commit suicide?"

Cameron nodded grimly.

Hedrick sat at the small table in his hotel room. He reached across the table and took a gun in his hand. He slowly turned it over in his hand, examining it. He looked up to the mirror on the wall. In his eyes, grief and rage danced deep within. *How could this be,* he puzzled. *Why is she with him?*

He looked up to the ceiling. "You haven't won," he said aloud, "not this time."

Edmund stepped into the dining room to find a sobbing Kaitty, arms folded on the table, head on top of them. He walked up to her and placed himself in a chair by her. He laid his hand on her shoulder. She lifted her tear-stained face to look him in the eyes.

"Not very good first impression, huh?" she joked.

Edmund gently pulled her to him, put his other arm around her, and let her cry in his chest.

Hedrick scurried around the room, searching in dresser drawers, the closet, everywhere. He grabbed different items of need and shoved everything into a small duffle bag. Grabbing his keys, he headed out of the hotel room. *This has to stop. No way will she do this to me. She'll pay for what she's done this time.*

Edmund carried Kaitty upstairs and laid her down in bed. She had cried herself to sleep in his arms. He was glad his military training had paid off away from duty. He pulled the covers over his wife, changed into his pajamas, and snuck back downstairs. He stepped out onto the back porch, barely lit at all on that cloudy night.

He looked up to the sky. Burying his face in his hands, he fell to his knees in the soft grass. He needed some solitude, to be in a place just long enough to pray in private.

His Uncle needed all the prayers he could get.

Hedrick drove recklessly through town. He unzipped the duffle bag and dug out the black gloves and ski mask he had brought. He put on the gloves and stuffed the ski mask into a smaller bag, along with duct tape, a bandana, and sat it with the baseball bat.

"I'll get back at you for doing this," he said aloud again to himself. "Nobody takes anything away from Hedrick John Lorenz, especially his pride!"

"God," he began, "please help my Uncle Hedrick. And please help my wife. She's so upset over this. Lord, why is it always me? I forget to do something simple and then someone else pays for it. Just—please help." Edmund heard thunder rumble in the distance. What was it about this night that didn't feel right?

Hedrick parked the van in front of the house and snuck around to the back, making sure that no one could see him from a nearby porch light. He saw Edmund there on his knees, talking upward to the sky.

So that's where I get all this God stuff from. My brother's been teaching them—more like preaching to them. He waited until Edmund's head was down and his eyes were closed. He quietly opened the wooden gate door and slowly approached from behind. His cover was blown when he missed seeing a stick on the ground. It snapped and it looked as though Edmund froze.

Hedrick held the bat in his hands, drew it back swiftly, and swung it with full force as Edmund looked around, striking at his head.

Edmund, kneeling, was thinking about his wife, his uncle, his parents, his unborn child, and how he and Kaitty were to be parents. He closed his eyes. His life was changing, and quickly. Before he knew it, he was engaged, then married, and now expecting a child.

My life is going too fast, he thought. *I need to be spending more time doing the important things instead of being at work all the time. I need more time with Kaitty.*

He felt rain sprinkling on his head and neck. He heard a twig crack behind him. He opened his eyes and stared at the ground. He heard running, then grunting. He turned to look behind him, but everything went black.

Hedrick watched his nephew collapse on the ground and he felt the rain start to come harder. He pulled Edmund's body to the darkest corner of the porch and hid him there. He gathered his things and let himself into the house.

It was dark. There was only a light on the stairs up to the second floor. Hedrick followed the light up the stairs. He looked down the hall to his right, then to the left. He heard a noise from an open door at the end of the left side of the hall; someone moving in bed. He slowly inched his way down the hall. He peered in through the open door and saw a lump in the bed move. He smiled to himself, quietly set down his small bag and bat, dug through it, and pulled out the bandana and duct tape. He pulled the ski mask from his pocket and shoved it on his head. He stood and progressed forward into the room while thunder warned of the on-coming storm.

Kaitty stirred from her slumber by a blast of thunder. And a creaking of floor boards startled her. Someone was in the room. What sounded like booted feet came closer and closer to her.

She half way sat up and leaned on one of her arms facing the window. She saw the reflection of a masked figure coming toward her. Her mouth was agape and she tried to let out a scream, but the intruder took a bandana that he held in his hand and tied it around her mouth. She hit the covers on the other side of the bed, trying to rouse Edmund. No one was there.

It was clear to her what was happening. And there was nothing she could do. Or was there?

Hedrick saw Kaitty begin to yell and tried to tie the bandana around her mouth. But in doing so, she bit him. He hit her across the face, making blood fly onto the wall and carpet. She fell to her knees in pain. He pinned her up against the wall and tied the bandana around her mouth.

"Now, if you try to make a sound, I will shoot you," he said, his head an inch from hers. She breathed heavily. "Now get up!"

Not doing what he had demanded, Hedrick yanked her to her feet by her arms. He quickly duct taped her hands together behind her back. "Let's go!"

He started shoving her out of the house. He quickly looked around. The coast was clear. He opened the back doors of the van and pushed Kaitty inside. He closed the doors and got in the driver's seat. He threw the smaller bag and bat into the seat next to him, shoved his hand into the duffle bag, and pulled out a gun.

He looked back to the squirming Kaitty, who lay on her stomach, blood oozing from her nose. She, helplessly, looked at him. He showed her the gun and said, "You try to make an attempt to escape or harm me, you'll get a bullet."

Chapter Eight

Edmund woke to a pain in his head. Though it hurt, he didn't grunt or move or open his eyes. *Where am I,* he thought. He heard whispers all around him.

"Cameron, I think he's waking up." He heard footsteps, breathing near his face, a hand holding his, and lips on his forehead. "Edmund?" she said. He slowly opened his eyes and saw his mother a foot from him and his father next to her. "Oh, Edmund."

He finally grunted in pain. His head felt like it was about to bust. "Wha—what happened to me?"

"We were hoping you could tell us," said Cameron. "One of your neighbors called the police and said they saw someone lying on the back porch. They said that they kept asking if he was alright, but never received an answer. The police came and hopped the fence. They checked you over and here we are."

Edmund sat up and looked around the room. "Where's Kaitty?"

Christine bit her lip and Cameron sighed.

"We...couldn't find her," he said.

Edmund sprang up out of the bed and onto his feet like a cat. "What!"

"Ed, calm down," pursued Christine. "Everything will be alright."

"I won't calm down 'til I find her!"

"Ed, you need to get back into that bed." He turned to see his brother standing in the doorway, clipboard in hand. "Sit," he said, pointing towards the bed. Edmund had to obey this time. He longed to know if Kaitty was alright.

Tyler looked down at the clipboard. "Now, you have a fractured skull, no brain—."

"I don't want to know about me! I just want to know where my wife is, if she's okay!"

"Ed, I know this must be hard on—."

"No you don't, Tyler! Your wife is safely at home with your kid while mine is missing, pregnant, and you won't let me out of this cursed bed to look for her!"

"We'll tend to you first, and then worry about Kaitty. No argument about it."

The door to the back of the van opened and rain came pouring in. Kaitty had fallen asleep and knew she could have been driven hours away from her home.

The man who had taken and driven her here stood there before her in the open doors. He reached his hand to the top of his head and pulled off the ski mask. She gasped when she saw the unmistakable face.

Hedrick laughed. "So, you thought you could get away with rubbing in my face the fact that my family's dead. Big mistake. Get up!"

He grabbed her by one of her tied arms, manhandling her out of the van. "Walk!"

She never knew a time she was more afraid than this. She could not keep it from showing. There she was, an eight month pregnant woman, taken from her own bed by her husband's uncle, thrown into the back of a van, threatened with a gun pointed at her, and now being forced into a creepy house/shelter by a man with a disturbing past.

As she slid a time or two in the mud, Kaitty didn't know what to do. Would he keep her in this place until she had the baby, then keep the child and raise it for himself? She tried to push such thoughts from her head. She could not worry about what could happen in a few weeks yet. She had to stay focused on what was happening then right before her or risk getting killed by this mad man. She knew she could only depend on God to get her and her unborn child out of this and back home where they belong.

"They found blood—in our room?"

Christine nodded tearfully. "Edmund, it'll be alright. God will deliver and keep her safe."

He wished he could weep, but he had to stay strong. How he wanted Kaitty, to hold her, to kiss her, and never let her go from his sight. He was scared of what could happen to her.

Kaitty was tossed into a cold cellar in the basement. The door slammed behind her as she lay on the floor, but she stood and, since she had been untied, pounded on the door with her fists. She began to cry.

She heard movement in a far corner behind her and turned to look into a pair of watery, brown eyes on a young, tearstained, terrorized face.

Edmund was told he could not take off the wrap around his head for another two weeks. But he was glad when he could get out of that confounded bed. He was headed home that day. Though, in going home, that meant being alone and constantly being reminded that Kaitty was not there.

He was driven home by his parents, one of whom said they would stay with him until they were sure he was level-headed and would not do anything crazy.

On the way there, Christine got a call. She opened her phone and said, "Hello?"

Edmund could hear a frantic woman talking rapidly on the other end. "What are you talking about, Mrs. Clint?...Calm down. Now, what happened?...Calm down, Mrs. Clint. It'll be alright. We're headed there. Keep all the windows and doors shut and locked until we get there."

She shut the phone and spoke to Cameron. "Head home."

"Why?" he asked.

She took a breath and said, "Jana's gone missing."

They had turned and sped to their house.

Edmund sat glued to his seat in shock. First his wife, then his little sister. Why would someone want them? What good would come out of having them? Ransom money?

The car came to a screeching halt in the driveway of the house. All three of them got out. Cameron ran to the door while Christine stayed by Edmund's side.

Cameron started banging on the door and yelled, "Mrs. Clint! Open the door!"

They heard the locks click and the door swung open. When Mrs. Clint was revealed, they saw a big black and blue spot on the right side of the woman's head.

"Mrs. Clint, we need to get you to the hospital."

"I'll be fine. I'm more worried about Jana."

"Mrs. Clint, you don't know how bad that could be," said Edmund. "I have a fractured skull 'cause of a blow to it. Yours is starting to bleed. Go with my mom to the hospital and get it checked out. Dad and I will stay here."

She reluctantly nodded. She let Christine put her arm around her, and they climbed into the car.

"Jan—?"

Jana quickly raised a finger to her lips. She shook her head and whispered, "They may not know we're related."

"One of them is your uncle. They know."

Kaitty looked at Jana's face, and then her eyes traveled up to the side of her forehead. There was a baseball sized, black and blue bruise on her head.

"What happened to you?"

"I'll explain later. Kaitty, what's going to happen to us?"

"I don't know. And I'm afraid to know why."

"We haven't done anything. Why would they be doing this to us?"

Kaitty shrugged. "We probably will never know."

What seemed like hours later, the door swung open. There stood two men; Hedrick and someone that must have been his accomplice.

"Take the little one," Hedrick ordered. "I get the trouble maker."

As his accomplice stepped into the light from a dusty window, he ran a hand through his messy red hair. A grin was set on his dirty, freckled face. He harshly grabbed Jana and shoved her out the door.

Once the accomplice had grabbed Jana, Hedrick came to Kaitty and grabbed her right arm.

"This way, my niece," he said gleefully.

He guided her out of the room gently. It made her even more uneasy.

They followed the others into an office looking room. The two captives were led to the front of a desk at the far end of the room. Hedrick took both girls by the arms and ordered his accomplice (whose name turned out to be Andy) to get the two chairs that sat to the side of the room and place them for the girls to sit in front of the desk. Andy did as told and set the chairs in place.

Hedrick told them to sit, but when they did not, Andy yelled, "He said sit!"

Frightened, the two finally followed the mad-man's orders.

Hedrick sat down behind the desk and began, "Now you—."

"Why did you bring us here?" blurted Kaitty.

Hedrick looked surprised that someone he had kidnapped would interrupt him. "Why?" he began. "Why did I snatch you? You want to know why? I'll tell you. You don't deserve my nephew! You'll go and break his heart, just like—."

He stopped his rant. He sat like a statue staring at Kaitty with his dark piercing eyes. He swallowed and said to Andy, "Take the little one to the cellar."

He had not looked to Andy when he spoke, but had kept his eyes firmly on Kaitty. She felt she was going to die.

Cameron called 911. In turn, they sent a team of FBI Investigators out to his house. They arrived and set out on finding evidence in the house.

The kidnapper was good at remaining anonymous. But they found a hair and finger prints in Jana's room. They had the evidence photographed, collected, and taken back to the Center. Only three out of the ten FBI agents remained to interview Mrs. Clint, who was back from the hospital, and tell the others of any information when it came.

The chief investigator talked with Edmund and Cameron while the other two agents interrogated Mrs. Clint.

Edmund didn't listen to the head agent. He just stared at him, wondering if he would ever hold Kaitty or Jana again, wondering why God would do that to them. He wondered if God was not what he thought He was.

Don't think that, he thought. *That's just Satan trying to get in your head. God is good. And this isn't His fault.*

He wished his heart was in that thought completely. Oh, how he longed for Kaitty! He wanted more than ever to cry for her. He knew it was wrong to think, but, when he found out who had taken Kaitty, he was going to kill him.

Andy shut the door behind him as he escorted Jana back to the cellar. Hedrick still sat in silence. He now gazed down at his legs, leaning on the desk with his arms.

"I would kinda like to know why I'm being held in this place." The words were out of her mouth before she knew it.

Hedrick looked up. Kaitty was startled when she'd seen tears in his eyes. "You want to know why?" he asked. "Because God broke my family! He wants to hurt me, and then I'll do the same to Him!"

"But you're doing this to your nephew, too!"

"Shut up you insolent girl! Do you think I care *who* I kill or *who's* loved ones I'll be taking away? I'm going to get back at Him for what He's done to my life. He let my wife and son die right before my eyes, even when I was faithful to Him. What excuse do you have for Him? You are a Lorenz after all. They *always* have a reason."

"I don't know why it happened, but it wasn't His doing!"

"I'm done with you," he said. He stood from his chair and yelled, "Andy! Take blonde out!"

Andy opened the door, strode in, and took her by the arm.

"You said you were a believer, but you're a fake!" she yelled as Andy pulled her to her feet.

"I want her out of my sight!"

"You can't run from Him *or* the truth!"

Hedrick came around the desk and punched Kaitty in the face. "That'll teach you not to speak disrespectfully to me! Andy, take care of her!"

"Excuse me a moment," said the chief agent as he took out his ringing cell phone. They listened to his side of the conversation.

"Agent Dean here.... Yeah, go on.... Who did it come up with?...Okay, I'll tell them. Thanks." He hung up.

"Well," he continued, "the results on the hair and finger prints came back. They told me that all of the evidence was traced to a guy named Andy Hander. This man has been on the FBI's '10 Most Wanted' list for sexual assault, battery, and murder for more than ten years now. I can't even begin to tell you how many have been affected by him."

Edmund was horrified. "After ten years you still haven't found him?"

"Don't worry; your house will be under careful observation until he is caught. Your last name is Lorenz, correct?"

Cameron nodded. The agent flipped to the back of his clipboard to the next available information slot. "Well, what do you know? The last person we helped out was an Edmund Lorenz!"

"That's me," said Edmund.

"Wait, you two are related?"

"Yes."

"What's your relation with both cases, Sir?"

"The first is my wife. The second is my little sister."

"Sir, I'm going to have to ask you to come to the FBI Center with me. Your relation with the cases is just a little suspicious."

"Why would I kidnap my own wife?"

"I don't know, Sir. Jealousy, control, money. But it's policy to take people with relations to the Center if it seems suspicious or they're related to more than one case."

"Dad." Edmund looked to his father for help, but Cameron just told him that he would bring someone down there.

Andy took Kaitty out of the office. Before throwing her into the cellar, he punched her a couple times in the face and once in the stomach.

Kaitty was pushed off her feet onto the cold, cement floor of the cellar. The door closed behind her. Someone was hurrying to her, but she didn't have the strength to look up.

"Kaitty—Kaitty, can you hear me?"

Kaitty did not move or make a sound. Jana pulled her over to the far side of the room, took a blanket that was sitting in a corner, and threw it over Kaitty. She started tending to her bloody nose.

Kaitty was too weak to move. *God, am I going to die here? Please, Lord, let me live long enough to see Edmund again.*

At the FBI Center, Edmund was led into an interviewing room. The agent said he would be back in a minute and left.

Once the door was shut, Edmund lost it. He broke down, crying. He slid off the chair, onto his knees, and began praying. Moments later, the agent came back in.

"Well," he said, "shall we—Sir, are you alright?"

Edmund lifted his head. The agent was kneeling in front of him. The agent pulled him up by the arm and sat him down in his seat. "Do you need me to call an ambulance?"

Edmund shook his head. "I'm sorry. It's just—I found out my wife was missing this morning while I was sitting in a hospital bed. Then, I'm headed home when I'm told that my little sister is also missing. I was just asking God to keep them safe."

"It'll be alright," the agent reassured. "That's what we're here for. Let's begin. Where were you last night when your wife went missing?"

"I was out in the backyard, unconscious."

"So you're saying that it wasn't you? Do you know who it was?"

"No. Do you think I would be here if I did? I'm innocent! Can't we just focus on trying to find her instead of who to blame!"

He was polite, yet, like all good FBI agents, he was stern. "Sir, this is part of how we find people. We have to figure out the who and the why to be able to locate missing people. Do you understand why this is important now?"

"I'm sorry. But if you knew me personally like my family does, you'd know that I am not the kind of person to do something like this!"

"But who isn't to say that a military man and his wife had some kind of argument that made one blow their top and the other disappeared?"

Edmund leaned closer across the table. "Understand this; I love my wife and I would give my life to protect her! That goes for my sister, too. Being a military man doesn't mean that I'm controlling or sadistic! Am...I...clear?"

The agent sighed. "Alright. Let's move on. What can you tell me about your wife? I need physical descriptions, health facts, all that you can give me."

After gaining control of himself again, he started. "She has mud-blond hair that comes down about mid-chest, hazel eyes—she's five-foot-four, age is twenty-one, will be twenty-two in August, name is Kaitty Lillian Lorenz, is allergic to pollen, and she's pregnant."

The agent stopped writing the information and looked up. "I never heard she was pregnant. How many months is she?"

"About eight."

"That's not good. Does she have any enemies that would like to get back at her for anything she might have done, intentionally or otherwise?"

"Not that I'm aware of."

"What happened the night she disappeared? Who saw her last besides you?"

"Well, the only people who saw her were my parents and my uncle."

"Names?"

"Parents' are Cameron and Christine Lorenz. My uncle is Hedrick Lorenz."

"What happened when they saw her?"

Edmund plunged into the short version of the past night. "It was at supper last night. My parents and Uncle came over and we just talked."

"About what?"

"Isn't that getting a little personal?"

"I'm sorry, Sir. It's part of my job routine."

Edmund told him about them talking about the wedding and why Hedrick couldn't come and how Kaitty had asked if he missed his family. "She heard that he lived in Chicago. She asked if his family missed him, and everyone went quiet. Hedrick got up and left."

As Edmund told the events, he talked slower, realizing what had taken place. "Oh, God, Uncle Hedrick!"

Chapter Nine

She woke to sobs. "No, Kaitty!" She felt a hand being placed in hers and tears falling onto her face. Kaitty slowly opened her eyes as the tears stopped falling on her. Jana sat, kneeling by her side. "God," she prayed aloud, "please don't take Kaitty away from us, at least not in this place. Please, Lord, heal her!"

Kaitty turned her head. Jana's head was bowed, her eyes were closed, and she was shaking. "Jana," she said, weakly.

Her head shot up. She had never looked more scared with her tear-stained cheeks. "Kaitty," she breathed. "You're alive."

"Of course I am. What made you think I wasn't?"

"Your breathing nearly stopped, and your pulse was faint. Kaitty, I thought Uncle Hedrick killed you! Does he know you're pregnant?"

"Yes."

"Well, then maybe you have a chance."

"How? He's already beaten me."

"He could keep you alive long enough to have the baby. You still have a month."

"But what if he doesn't? I can't bear the thought of losing the baby if I go. I want Ed to have him—or her."

"Well, I hope he doesn't do anything. But while you were out, I heard them yelling something about Hedrick carrying out his plan and that he was going to do it tonight."

The door burst open. Hedrick came bounding in. "Say your last prayer, Kaitty Lorenz!"

Edmund was running out of the Center, and when he burst through the front doors, he ran head-on into two men.

"So sorry, gentlemen!" He ran a few more paces before one of the men called out to him.

"Edmund, where're you going?"

He turned back around to the men and saw his father getting up from the pavement. Beside him was Edmund's first officer, Lieutenant Barnes.

"Captain, I came to help clear your name," said the Lieutenant.

"Thank you, Lieutenant, but my name has already been cleared. We know who it is."

"Who?" Cameron asked.

Edmund swallowed and said, "Uncle Hedrick."

Hedrick dragged Kaitty into the same room she had been in earlier. He threw her to the floor, slammed the door shut, and turned to look at her. "Now," he said, "I've had something taking from me, now it's your turn."

She remained silent.

After a few moments, Hedrick lost it. He jumped on her, knocking her flat, punched her in the face, and then held her pinned by the arms, but she kicked him in the crotch.

After grunting in pain, he said, "You have pushed my patience too far, girl!" He looked over to the door and yelled, "Andy, get in here!"

The door flew open. Andy quickly stepped in and shut it again. Kaitty's heart was in her throat.

Hedrick pulled her to her feet by the shirt, spun her around, and let go. She landed in Andy's arms. He held her with her back to him, giving Hedrick a clear shot.

Hedrick strode up to her and punched her in the stomach. Andy released her, letting her fall to the ground. She sat on her legs, doubled over. Andy kicked her in the face, knocking her to her side in a fetal position, covering her face with her right hand, holding her stomach with the other.

Hedrick came over and began kicking her in the stomach repeatedly.

Back in the cellar, Jana heard kicks, screams, yells, and cries. She heard Hedrick yell, "This is what you get! It's what you deserve!"

She cried for Kaitty. What could she do? She heard her mother's voice in the back of her mind.

Pray, it said.

She prayed hard that God would protect Kaitty and keep her and the baby from harm.

"Where do we start?" asked Cameron.

"We need to have the FBI helping, Captain," said Lieutenant Barnes. "That's all I know."

"C'mon, Ed. We'll go in and see what can be done."

They filed into the FBI Center. The man that had interviewed Edmund came bounding to them.

"We've entered the name and info onto the computer," the agent said. "We've sent search crews to his house and to the hotel he had been at last night. They will get back to me with anything they come up with. Are you sure it was Hedrick Lorenz?"

"Positive," said Edmund. Then, to his dad, "Who knows what he'll do to her. You said yourself that he was suicidal! He could also be murderous, could he not?"

Cameron paused. "It'll be fine, son." The fact that he could not reply any more than that made fear rise in Edmund's heart. Fear for his wife, his sister, and his baby. Why would God allow something like this happen to them?

"Come and wait in my office," said the agent. "They should get back to us soon."

Kaitty moaned. What had happened to her? Her stomach felt like it would burst with the pain. Her head throbbed and she could barely breathe. She opened her eyes, staring at a cement ceiling. The room was cold and dark. She pulled herself into an upright sitting position and leaned against the wall. Where was she?

Something moved beside her. She turned to look at another person. The person looked up and said, "Kaitty, you're alright!"

The person got up and started toward her. Kaitty tried scooting backward, but, in the attempt, her leg exploded into unbearable pain. She let out a quick yelp and stopped, holding her right leg with both hands.

"Kaitty, be quiet! You don't want them to wake!"

Kaitty looked around the room. There was no one else in there. She turned back to the person and pointed to herself. The person looked confused. "Kaitty, it's me, Jana."

Was she supposed to know this person? Kaitty wondered if this person who called herself "Jana" was delirious.

"Do you remember me?" she pressed. Kaitty shook her head. "Do you know who you are?" She shook her head again. Jana looked like she would cry. "What has Hedrick done to you?"

Edmund, Cameron, Lieutenant Barnes, and the agent had waited in that office for a good hour before the agent's phone rang.

"Have you found anything?...Okay, nothing suspicious at the house. What about the hotel?...Around what time?...All right, thank you." He hung up. He turned to the others and said, "There was a witness at the hotel that said he saw someone who fits Hedrick Lorenz's description to the T. One of the agents showed him a photo and the man confirmed him as the one he saw the previous night. They searched the room, found it a mess, but there was nothing suspicious there besides an address book they found."

"How was it suspicious?" asked Edmund.

"One of the locations is titled 'S.H.' and 'H.O.'. We assume these mean sa—."

"Safe House and Hide Out." The agent looked to Edmund with a confused look. "I remember him telling us about his 'Safe House' and 'Hide Out' that he used in case of 'bad weather', and this sure is bad weather right now."

"Do you know where it's at?"

"He didn't have it listed?"

"No. This is a criminal we're talking about here, not some old, trustworthy friend. Most criminals such as him are smarter than we think in this area of crime."

"Right, well, he said it was out in the country in some wooded area somewhere. He let slip that it was east of my parent's house."

"Well, that helps the search. We know an area to look. We're bringing in two agents from Georgia. The names are Rob Anderson and Claire Smith. They'll help with the search."

"Why do you have to bring people in? Don't you have enough?"

"These are the best agents in the U.S.. They've received awards for 'Best FBI Agent' several times, even though they're on the young side. I've met them and I think they're wonderful—in business and just regular people."

"I guess we'll have to take your word on it."

"Well, there's nothing more that can be done tonight, Edmund," said Cameron, "so let's get you home. Your old bedroom should be ready for you by now."

After telling Kaitty some things about herself, Jana asked "Do you understand what I've told you?" Kaitty nodded. "There's one more thing."

"What?"

"You know how babies are born and all that right?" She nodded again. "Well, you are."

She cocked her head and asked, "Are what?"

"Pregnant."

Kaitty closed her eyes. Even with the memory loss, she still knew that that was not a place for a pregnant woman to be. "How many months?"

"A little over eight."

She felt like she could die. "Jana, why can't I remember anything? I can't remember what my husband looks like, I don't know where I live, I don't remember my family—I couldn't even remember I was pregnant! Jana, I'm scared."

"I know, so am I."

The cellar was cold, Kaitty could not remember, Jana was scared, and they didn't know what was going to happen to them. Jana knew matters where beginning to fall into her hands and that she had to get Kaitty out of there no matter what it took.

As Edmund ate his supper in bed, a feeling of uneasiness overcame him. He felt the need to pray. He put down his plate, threw the blankets off him, and eased himself out of bed. Kneeling, he began to pray.

Lord, I'm worried. Has Kaitty been hurt? Jana? Lord, I ask of You only one thing: please keep them safe.

He climbed back into bed, grabbed a newspaper off of the bedside table, and began reading. A few moments later, Christine came in.

"Edmund, you've barely touched your supper. Are you feeling alright?" She put her hand to his forehead.

"I'm fine, mom. I'm just not hungry."

"Edmund, this isn't like you. You wouldn't give up meatloaf for anything! Now, what's wrong?" She sat on the edge of the bed, waiting for his reply.

Edmund took a deep breath and began. "I'm worried. I mean—Uncle Hedrick took my pregnant wife and little sister! That's not the Hedrick I remember. Do you remember that time when I was thirteen and I told Uncle Hedrick that I was going outside when he was watching us? It had been an hour since he saw me last, so he came out and went looking for me. He kept looking around on the edge of the timber for me, thinking I was in there. I finally heard him, climbed to the doorway of that old tree house of dad's, and told him I was over there. He came running over to me as I was climbing down the ladder, lifted me off it, and hugged me so tightly I thought he would've broken my back. He was so worried 'cause he couldn't find me. He told me later that he was afraid I might've wondered off into the timber. 'You're not little,' he told me, 'and you're not that young, but you're my nephew and just a boy, and I love you.' He cared that much about me then, but why not now?"

"Honey, I know what you're feeling and what you're going through, but Hedrick is a very disturbed man right now. Aunt Alibbiea and your cousin Johnny were killed about a month ago by a drunk driver, and he feels guilty for it because he was driving."

"Why?"

"I don't have the answer for everything. But God does. And if you don't know, that's probably how God wants it to be."

"Well, why can't he get some help? Don't people like him go to psychiatrists?"

"'People like him?' Edmund Gabriel Lorenz, he's your uncle, and nothing less."

"I know, but everyone else who's gone through this sort of thing has gone to one. Why shouldn't he?"

"We've tried to get him to go, but your uncle is one stubborn man. He kept telling us that he just needed time and he would be alright. And you know your uncle; once he's made up his mind, there's nothing you can do to change it.

"All we can do right now is pray. Pray for Kaitty and Jana's safety—and that Hedrick heals. It hurts, I know.

And I know why you wouldn't want to pray for him, but it may help him."

Edmund blew up. "Mom, he kidnapped my wife and my sister! How do you know how I feel? Huh? Why should I pray for a man that's taken away part of my family? Tell me, why?"

"Edmund Lorenz! Jana isn't just your sister, she's my daughter! And your wife is like another daughter of my own!" She stopped herself and took a deep breath. "I'm sorry. But this hasn't hurt just you. It's hurt this entire family. But we have to be strong, especially you."

Edmund didn't respond. He sat there, leaning against the headboard of his bed, staring at the newspaper lying on top of the covers. Christine rose, took the plate from the bedside table, and walked to the door. "I'm sorry, mom," his whispered.

She turned. "It's alright. We're all going through a crisis and it'll affect our moods sometimes." She walked out into the hall. "I'll make sure you aren't disturbed. You need to get to bed. It's almost midnight."

"If I'm not up by ten, wake me."

"Alright then. Goodnight, Edmund."

"'Night, mom."

She turned off the light and closed the door behind her, leaving him with only the lamp for light. He unfolded the *Red Oak Happenings* newspaper. He knew that whatever was on the front page was the most interesting thing in there. He looked at the first headline. It read:

Officer Accuses Man of Selling Drugs While Picking Up His Turkey

Chase Goodmen was spotted at 512 Park Avenue by Mark Hall, a Red Oak police man. The officer was on call of a reported drug house, that of which being 512 on Park Avenue. Officer Hall saw Mr. Goodmen park in front of the house and get out of the car. That is when Hall pulled up around to the front of the house and called out to the young man, asking what he was doing out that late.

Goodmen replied that he was getting his turkey from his grandfather's freezer in the carport and that he was not going inside or talking to the residents. Hall asked him if he was getting drugs. Goodmen's reply was, "This house is not a drug house."

Hall circled the block and parked back at his station and watched as Goodmen took a bag to his car. He swung back around and asked what he had in the bag. Goodmen replied that it was his turkey. Hall asked to see it. Reluctantly, Goodmen obliged the officer and opened the bag. Hall cleared it as a turkey and let Goodmen go on his way.

Hall gave a defense of, "It was my job to assure the citizens of this and neighboring towns that every suspicious person was watched carefully so there would be no drug dealing or thievery. I was simply doing my job."

Only time will tell if Officer Hall was right to do such.

Edmund chuckled after finishing the article, shaking his head, and said, "Only in Red Oak."

Edmund woke at half past eight the next morning. He got up, put his robe on over his pajamas, and trudged downstairs. He smelled the aroma of pancakes and bacon as he entered the living room, then into the kitchen. Cameron was seated at the table; Christine was busy cooking.

"'Morning," said Edmund.

Cameron put down the day's newspaper and looked up to Edmund. "'Morning, Edmund. Sleep well last night?"

"Yeah." He sat down next to him and his mother spoke.

"Breakfast will be done in a few. Do you want something to drink?"

"Orange juice, please." She swept over to the fridge. He spoke again to his father. "Anything interesting in there today?"

Cameron looked over the top of the paper. He folded it and threw it onto the table in front of Edmund, saying, "Look for yourself."

He picked up the newspaper and unfolded it to look at the front page. He could not believe his eyes.

Two Local Women Kidnapped

Last Sunday, two women were taken from their homes. Jana Lorenz, age 18, and Kaitty Lorenz, age 21, were kidnapped in the cover of night. Edmund Lorenz, the brother of Jana and the husband of Kaitty, was questioned by the FBI the next day after he was released from the hospital with a head injury. When asked if he had anything to do with the kidnappings, he denied all charges saying, "Why would I kidnap my own wife and sister?"

Authorities questioned him further, asking things like, "Does (Kaitty) have any enemies that would harm her?" and "What happened the night before (Kaitty) was taken?" Lorenz answered saying, "My parents and uncle came over for supper." He went on to say that they began talking and Kaitty asked about the uncle's family. The uncle (identified as Hedrick Lorenz) ran from the scene. Edmund Lorenz knew, after talking with the FBI, that his uncle had been the one who kidnapped his wife.

The FBI ran the information provided by Lorenz and sent search crews to Hedrick Lorenz's house out in Chicago and the hotel he had checked into here in Red Oak. Witnesses say they saw Hedrick Lorenz leave the hotel late at night with a duffle bag in his hand. He did not turn his room key in and when FBI agents searched the room, they found it in a mess. The only thing they could find was an address book that had two names for a location that had no address. "S.H." and "H.O." were listed in the back of the book. Edmund Lorenz was told this and he immediately confirmed what FBI agents speculated. Lorenz said, "Safe House and Hide Out." He said that his uncle had let slip that the "Safe House/Hide Out" was east of his parent's home in Council Bluffs.

The FBI is bringing in two agents from Georgia and they will help with the search. They are currently looking east from Lorenz's parents' home out in the country in the woods. No word yet on any findings.

What has caught the attention of the FBI on this one especially is that Kaitty Lorenz is eight months pregnant and that the accomplice was identified at the crime scene of Jana Lorenz's house as none other than Andy Hander, one of the FBI's "Top Most Wanted". He has been committing crimes for more than ten years, but they have yet to catch him. People are asked to be cautious for he has been charged for sexual assault, battery, and murder.

There is a photograph of Hander and one of Hedrick Lorenz at the bottom of this page that the FBI is asking you to keep, study, and watch out for them. If you have any information on the whereabouts of Andy Hander, Hedrick Lorenz, Kaitty Lorenz, or Jana Lorenz, please call the FBI center immediately.

Edmund studied the picture of his wife and the one of Andy Hander. He nearly broke down thinking about how his wife and little sister could be murdered. He knew he had to trust the Lord and pray for their safety, but he wished he could do more.

Kaitty had tried to fall asleep that night, but she couldn't with knowing what condition she was in and where she was. Jana tried her best to comfort her. But nothing worked until she remembered Psalm 23.

And she recited it to her. "Even though I walk through the valley of the shadow of death, I will fear no evil, for you are with me; your rod and your staff, they comfort me."

Kaitty looked confused. "What does it mean?"

"It means though we may be facing death, we shouldn't fear anything, for the Lord is with us through all of it. He is also known as the Good Shepherd, and that is what it refers to when it says 'your rod and your staff'. 'Your rod and your staff' will comfort us and keep us safe, basically meaning God will watch over us. We just have to put our faith in Him."

She nodded slightly. Then she asked, "You're younger than me, right?" Jana nodded. "I find it kinda weird then that you're quoting—ah—what was it called?"

"Scripture."

"Yah, weird that you're quoting Scripture to me. Jana, will I ever remember the things I've forgotten?"

"Well, I don't know. But I'm thinking positive."

Kaitty was upset, then she grabbed her stomach gently when she felt movement, and she heard a grumble. "You alright?" asked Jana.

She nodded. "I'm just a little hungry. Don't they ever feed us?"

"Kaitty, we're their hostages. They don't care if we starve."

"Oh, right. But didn't you say one of them was our uncle?"

"My uncle, your uncle-in-law. But that doesn't matter to him either 'cause he's the one who planned all this."

They were both silent for a minute, then Kaitty spoke. "Jana, if we are God's people and God is the shepherd, then are we his sheep?"

She sighed, and then answered, "Yes."

"Then we are God's lost sheep."

Chapter Ten

"You probably don't remember, but there's a story about a lost sheep. This shepherd was tending his one hundred sheep. He counted them all to find that one was missing. So he left the other ninety-nine sheep to look for that one lost sheep. He searched for a long time until he finally found him. When he did, he picked it up and carried it back to the rest of the herd."

Kaitty sat thinking for a moment, and then asked, "Is God looking for us?"

Jana thought on the question for a moment and answered, "I think He knows where we are. The story is usually told to show that God is looking for people who haven't asked to have their sins taken away, like Hedrick."

"So He's not looking for us?"

"He knows where we're at. We've asked for His forgiveness and He's forgiven us. He doesn't need to look for us. In this situation, God is protecting us."

She was doubtful. If there was a God and He was protecting them, then why were they in this mess?

Edmund didn't know what to do. He hadn't felt like doing anything except helping to look for Kaitty and Jana. But he could not do that considering they had not gotten any new information on their location.

He decided to head to the Center to wait for any news. He wondered when the two agents would come. They sounded like nice people, and he could not wait to have more people searching for Kaitty and Jana. He began to worry over them again. Are they hurt? *Who knows?* he thought. Are they frightened? *Most definitely!* Are they alive or are they dead? *Again, who knows?* He knew he had to keep positive. He knew he had to trust God.

Edmund reached the Center and jogged inside. Once in, he stopped by the front desk to ask if there were any new leads.

"I'm sorry, Mr. Lorenz, there's none that I've heard of." He nodded to the lady and headed on his way. He turned and started for the stairs, but was stopped by someone calling him.

When he looked around, he saw a woman walking towards him. She was about 5`2 with long, dark hair, and green eyes. The heels of her shoes echoed softly through the hall as they hit the marble floor with each step. She wore skinny jeans and a tank-top that, to Edmund, was a little too revealing.

"And what do we have here?" she said. "What's a handsome man like you walking around here for?"

He was repulsed of this tramp. He had to avert his eyes from her. Her tank-top was much too revealing. "I'm sorry, Miss, but I have somewhere to be." He started walking to the stairs again when the woman grabbed his arm. She pulled him over to the hallway leading to the bathrooms and pinned him against the wall. Once she had him there, she kissed him full in the mouth.

"What do you think you're doing?" he yelled, pushing her away.

"Oh, don't pretend you don't like it." Her words were so soft and calm it made Edmund's stomach turn. "Tonight, maybe you and I could have dinner at a fancy restaurant, check into a hotel, and then we can be our own FBI Agents, hmm?"

Edmund didn't know what was worse: his wife and sister missing, or a tramp kissing him and then wanting to go to a hotel and "play Agents." His stomach turned when she said it and even more when he thought of it. "Look, I don't know what your problem is, but I'm married and—."

"Your wife doesn't have to know. It'll be our little secret."

She moved in to kiss him again, but he would not allow it. "Get away from me! I would never betray my wife—especially with a tramp like you!"

He finally made his escape. Instead of going up to the next floor, he went into the restroom down that hallway. He locked the door, stepped over to the sink, and splashed water onto his face. Would God be angry that someone had kissed him, but he had not wanted it? He got on his knees and prayed, asking Him for forgiveness and asked Him to help the woman. When he finished, there was a pound on the door.

"I haven't got all day!"

Edmund unlocked the door, and apologized to the man.

"Next time, don't take so long."

Edmund, at last, headed up to the second floor and into Agent Craig Dean's office. When he walked in, two people were sitting in front of his desk.

"Ah, this is Mr. Lorenz. Mr. Lorenz, this is Rob Anderson and Claire Smith, the two agents from Georgia."

When Edmund saw Claire Smith, he about lost his breakfast. It was the same tramp that tried to hit on him. He wanted to leave the room, but decided otherwise. He shook hands with Rob Anderson, who had stood up to greet him, but avoided Claire Smith altogether. And he saw she now wore a black jacket over her showing top.

Then Anderson spoke, "This is my fiancée, Claire." Edmund wanted to puke. "We're so sorry about your wife and sister."

"Thank you. I just hope they're found soon. Did they tell you about my wife?" Anderson shook his head. "She's eight months pregnant with our first."

"Oh my," said Anderson. Edmund thought he saw Claire move at the mention of him being a father soon. He also noticed that she now wore an engagement ring on her left hand. He knew it had not been there before.

"Alright," said Agent Craig, "let's get down to business. Now, we're looking for a hide out somewhere east of Cameron Lorenz's house. We've had—."

"Sorry to interrupt, but quick question," interrupted Anderson. "Is Cameron Lorenz related to Edmund here?"

"He's my father," answered Edmund. Anderson nodded.

"As I was saying, we've had people searching out there yesterday, but we're coming up with nothing. We don't know if it'll be underground or visible above, but we're searching very carefully. Now, I trust both of you will look at a map of the east part from Mr. Lorenz's house so that you'll know the area. So let's get to work on the search. And, Edmund, why don't you head home and take it easy, especially with that head trauma you received."

It was noon, Kaitty was hungry, scared, injured. She wondered what would become of her, whether she would get out alive or be killed by her capturers. She knew they would not bring them food. They'd rather see them starve to death than feed them like they were guests.

Kaitty looked to Jana who was leaning against the wall, head hanging to the left, eyes closed. She didn't want to wake her, but she was lonely and scared. She heard movement above her head, then voices. But where were they coming from?

She looked around the room, past Jana, then to her left. There she saw a vent near the floor. She slowly and painfully crawled over to it and listened.

"The FBI is too stupid to find us."

"They've put our pictures in the paper, told people to keep and study them, and you're saying that they won't find us! They have flyers with our hostages' pictures on every light pole in three counties! The FBI might be stupid, but my brother and nephew aren't! They'll find us."

"Now you sound like you don't want to get back at anyone. What's wrong with you, Hedrick? You're a softy!"

"What's wrong with *me*? Last night, I was awoken by a scream. I went down there with a bat to beat the crap out of whoever yelled, and I heard Jana asking Kaitty if she knew who she was! I stayed longer to listen, thinking I would beat them up, and Jana starts telling Kaitty all this Bible stuff. The one I remember the most was the one about the lost sheep."

"Oh, yeah, I think I know that one. This boy watched his sheep, one wandered off, got itself killed by a wolf. And the boy never found it and killed himself." Andy gave a chuckle.

"Andy, this isn't funny! I'll tell you the story, seeing that you don't know it." And he did. Afterward, he said, "Kaitty asked if God was looking for them. Jana explained how they weren't lost like the story points out, but that you and I were. She told her that He was protecting them, and she quoted Scripture before that.

"'Even though I walk through the valley of the shadow of death, I will fear no evil, for you are with me; your rod and your staff, they comfort me.'"

Kaitty heard Hedrick crying. Then he said, "They remind me—of my wife. She would always find something in her Bible that suited a situation and read it to me and my son. Little Johnny—he loved everything about church. He—even asked Alibbiea if he could go to the adult's class. She promised to take him to the one the next day. I drove them, picked them up two hours later, and headed home." He stopped and, even from down in the cellar, Kaitty felt the uneasiness. "That's when the drunk ran a red light and—killed them." He stopped again. "That's why I hate church people, 'cause if it wasn't for that freaking class, my wife and son would still be with me today!"

"Relax, man. Don't they believe in that 'Heaven and Hell' thing?"

"Yes. And I know what you're going to ask. I know they're in Heaven, but I'm angry 'cause He took them from me!"

"'He'? He who?"

"He, who, God!"

"You're a believer?"

"I believe He's real, but that doesn't mean I'm like my wife. If you haven't noticed, I've done things that even God would call crimes. Kidnapping, lying, beating up a woman. I'm not exactly 'right' with God."

"To get off that subject, what do we do about Miss Scripture and Mrs. No Brain? They're probably hungry."

Hedrick looked to him. "Now look who's the softy! You're on the FBI's 'Top Most Wanted' for sexual assault, battery, and murder, and you're thinking about feeding two captives!"

Before Andy could answer, someone called from outside, using a blow horn, saying, "You are surrounded! Come quietly and we won't shoot!"

Edmund was racing in the FBI Center. He had to catch up to Claire Smith. He had a lot to say about her actions. *No way am I just going to stand by and let her continuously do this and ruin other families.*

He was on the second floor at the stairs looking down in search of her. There she was, standing dead center, doing something with her hands. When he looked closer, he saw that she was taking off her ring. She put it in her pocket and started off after a youthful man. She was about to do the same as she had done with him. Edmund would not let it happen.

He raced down the stairs, three at a time. Trotting, he grabbed the back of her shirt and started to pull her in the opposite direction of the man to an empty hall. This time, he pinned her against the wall.

"You are one sick woman, Claire Smith! I don't know how your mind works, but I can tell you this: you will not fraternize with other men when you're engaged while I'm around! And I can guess your fiancé doesn't know you're doing this, right?"

"I can't stay tied to one man forever—."

"So he doesn't know. Well, maybe I should just tell him what you said to me so he's not making a big mistake by marring you!"

He began to walk away, but Claire shoved him against the wall. "You tell him and I swear to God you'll be sorry!"

"First, don't use His name in vain, and second, you try to do me harm and you'll be in jail *before* you can swear."

"So, you're one of *those* people, huh?"

"If you mean Christian, then yes."

"Well, no matter. My offer still stands. I can change your whole mind about this situation—."

"I don't think so. You know what I think of you and I'm not the least bit interested."

"Next you're going to tell me I need Jesus."

"Well, not now because you just said it yourself."

"Well, if there is a 'God', then why is your wife missing? Hmm? Why didn't 'God' protect her? Why is she not here with you? Tell me, is that the loving 'God' you people always talk about?"

He began to reply, but then he thought about it. Was she right? Was there even really a God? He had grown up in church, but what if it was not true?

"*Edmund…*"

Where was he? He couldn't see a thing. It was like he was in a giant rain cloud. Where had the FBI Center gone?

"*Why do you doubt my existence?*"

"Who are you? Where are you?"

"*I am your Lord God Almighty. You do not see Me because you are too far from Me to be able to see My light. Why do you listen to the words of the nonbeliever?*"

"Because what if she's right? How do you love if my wife is missing? How do I know that this whole thing isn't just a figment of my imagination?"

"*Child, you say that I could not love because of evil in your life. You claim this experience on imagination instead of truth. You are close to living in complete darkness. That is what you see around you.*"

"Please, tell me why my wife is missing!"

"Patience, child. You will know in time why things have happened. But only if you trust in Me..."

"Hey, Lorenz, are you alright?" Someone shook him. "Hey, come on. Wake up—Hey, someone call an ambulance! He's not coming to!"

"No, no, I'm alright." Edmund sat up from the floor. *What just happened?*

Rob looked him in the eyes. "Are you sure?" Edmund nodded. "We have your wife's location."

"Mr. Lorenz," said Agent Craig, "we've found the hide out. It's surrounded and more agents are headed out there as we speak."

"Have they gotten my wife and sister out?"

"No, but they have high-powered weapons pointed 360 degrees around the place."

"Well, what are we waiting for? Let's go!"

Hedrick did not know what to do. He had never anticipated that the FBI would come then on that day, a little more than 24 hours after he and his accomplice kidnapped Kaitty and Jana.

He had an idea. He ran down to the cellar and prepared himself for a fight.

Kaitty was startled when she heard thumping footsteps coming down the stairs. The door burst open. The noise woke Jana. Andy Hander appeared behind it.

Hedrick said from behind Andy, "You take the Little One."

Andy didn't hesitate. He went straight for Jana and Hedrick for Kaitty. Andy yanked Jana up onto her feet and shoved her out the door. Hedrick slowly strode over to Kaitty. He grabbed her right arm and pulled her up. She tried to balance all her weight on her left leg, but that was not possible when Hedrick started to make her walk. She took one step with her broken leg and yelled.

Hedrick hit her across the face with the back of his hand, making her fall. "Not a peep out of you!"

He pulled her up again and she limped along in pain, not daring to make a sound, though her leg hurt and tears streamed down her face.

He pushed her up the stairs, turned her left, and they walked into the living room. Jana had her hands tied behind her back, mouth duct taped, and was kneeling parallel to the couch. Hedrick sat Kaitty down beside her and did the same process to her as Andy had to Jana.

And the bullhorn sounded again. "Hedrick Lorenz, Andy Hander, come out with your hands up, unarmed, and this can all be settled!"

Hedrick looked to Andy and said, "You watch them. I'm gonna confront them."

"How?" Andy asked. He turned as Hedrick started walking towards the staircase that led from the main floor to the upper floor.

"The balcony up in the bedroom. I'll walk out, confront them, and walk back in. Simple as that. This will end tonight, whether I get my wife back or not!" And he hurried up the stairs.

"Wait! Did you just say 'get my wife back'? She's dead, Hedrick!"

Hedrick turned left twice on the second floor and then to his right into a bedroom. First he went over to the dresser, opened the top drawer, and pulled out a hand gun. Then he strode to the balcony. Opening the doors, he stepped out. All around the front of the house were police, cars, ambulances, fire trucks, and high powered guns pointed at the house. A policeman with a bullhorn saw Hedrick come out and began to confront him.

"Hedrick Lorenz, come quietly and no one will be hurt!"

"I'm not coming out, and neither are the hostages unless they're dead!" He held up the gun.

"We will break down the door if you don't come out! We don't want any bullets flying!"

"Then let me do what I need to do for myself!" He quickly stepped back inside and went to the bedroom doorway. "Andy, bolt the door and put the desk in the hallway in front of it! Now!" He went back to the balcony.

The officer spoke again. "Don't shoot anyone! Surrender and this can be worked out!"

Edmund's heart was pounding. They had found the hide out, but there was no word on the hostages. A police officer called over the radio.

"This is Agent Craig, over."

"Lorenz has stepped out onto the second floor balcony and is making contact with one of our guys, over."

"Ten-four, what is he saying?"

There was a pause. "Our man said if he came quietly, no one would be shot...He replied that he wasn't coming out, and same with the hostages, unless they're dead. And he's holding a gun.

"Our man has just told him that we would break down the door and that we didn't want bullets flying. Lorenz said 'Then let me do what I need to do for myself'.

"He has just gone back in...and he's back on the balcony. He is still refusing to come out."

"What's the status on the hostages?"

"We've not heard any shots, which may be a good sign. We're almost certain that nothing has happened just yet. He said they would only come out if they were dead, which must mean they're still alive. We know no more than that."

"Roger that, keep me posted. Headed to the scene. Over and out."

He clipped his radio piece back on its holder and continued to drive, lights flashing. He gave a quick side glance at Edmund and asked, "Are you alright, son?"

Edmund was sweating. For all they knew, Kaitty and Jana could be as good as dead right now. "Just worried about them."

Sitting in the back with Claire, Rob said, "It'll be alright."

"Thanks."

Kaitty watched as Andy ran to lock the door and pull a heavy desk to it, blocking any way in or out of it. Things were getting even more chaotic. She heard the conversation between the man with the bullhorn and Hedrick. She was hopelessly scared when he said that she and Jana would only get out if they were dead. She hoped that it would not end that way.

Hedrick came down the stairs holding two revolvers and a large rifle in his hands. Andy came back to the living room and asked, "What are we doing with those? I thought we weren't killing them."

"Times have changed, Andy." He thrust one of the revolvers into his hand. "We'll shoot them to where they won't die instantly."

"Where do we shoot?"

Hedrick looked to the two of them and thought. "You shoot her in the side of the stomach. I'll shoot blonde in the chest."

"But won't that—."

"Don't question me, Andy! Just do it!"

A devious smile appeared on Andy's face. He and Hedrick took aim at the two helpless women.

Hedrick whispered, "Revenge is now."

Hedrick's heart was pounding when he took aim with the rifle. He pointed the gun straight for Kaitty's chest. She breathed heavily. He could not believe what he was about to do. This was it. No more games. This was the end.

He turned to Andy and said, "On three. One…two…" He looked back at his target and whispered, "I loved you, yet you ran away from me."

It was time for revenge to take its place. "…Three." The triggers were pulled. Jana fell backwards, Kaitty, the same. Hedrick pulled the trigger one last time. The bullet entered Kaitty's right shoulder. There were screams and yells from outside.

"Guns were fired! Guns were fired! Get up there and break down the door!"

There was the sound of heavy footsteps coming to the door. They started banging on the door, trying to take it down. Hedrick stood over his victim and watched as blood filled her shirt. He looked into her face. *What have I done? What was I thinking? She wasn't my wife! I've killed my nephew's wife!*

"Agent C, shots were fired! I repeat, shots *were* fired!"

"Who shot and who was shot?"

"The shots came from inside the house. We don't know who has been shot yet. The men are lining up to break down the door."

"We're pulling into the drive. Over and out."

Edmund was frantic. The scene was not what he wanted to see. Ambulances, fire trucks, police, and men trying to break down the door lined the perimeter around the house. Once the car was parked, he ran to help the police at the door. The lock on it broke, but the door would not budge. They began pushing it in with all their might until they were able to fit in. Four of the men went to handcuff Hedrick and Andy. Two stayed at the door, pushing a desk that was placed behind it out of the way. Edmund ran to two bodies on the floor. He saw bullet holes in their shirts and he began to think they were dead. He went to Jana first.

"Jana – Jana, it's me, Edmund."

She opened her eyes to look at him and she breathed, "John 16—33." She could scarcely speak. He could just make out what she was whispering. She whispered something else. "K-Kaitt-y. She—shot—dead."

Edmund understood what she was trying to say. He put his focus on Kaitty. "Kaitty, sweetie, it's me. Wake up."

His heart was in his throat as he waited for her to respond. He waited and waited, but she never moved or blinked an eye and her chest hardly moved. She was slowly slipping away.

He was not about to let his wife die. "Help! Help! They're shot!"

Paramedics came running in to them at last. He moved to where he knelt behind them as the paramedics grabbed Jana and strapped her to a gurney. "This is my wife. Please, you've got to save her!"

The man who stayed examined her wounds and told Edmund to help get her on the second gurney. Then he told him to get in front of the gurney and help push it out the door. Edmund did as told.

Once they were out of the house, another paramedic came up and took Edmund's place, pushing Kaitty to an empty ambulance.

"We're going to need you to come along, Sir," said the first paramedic. Edmund nodded and jumped into the back of the ambulance. He sat next to one of the paramedics. The doors were closed and someone hit them twice with his fist to signal to the driver it was clear to go. The driver took off, following the first ambulance to the nearest hospital.

Kaitty's face was getting paler by the second. The paramedics placed an oxygen mask on her to keep her breathing. The first man pulled down towels from a cabinet and handed one to Edmund, telling him to put it over the wound on Kaitty's chest. "I need you to apply pressure to stop the bleeding," the paramedic said. He did. The first man took the other towel and placed it on Kaitty's shoulder.

"Does she have any medical issues?" the first asked. Edmund shook his head. The man looked up to him. "How many months along is she?"

"Eight."

The man dug out his stethoscope and put it to Kaitty's chest. He listened to her heartbeat and shook his head. Edmund's heart began to race again. "Her heart is faint." He took out a different oxygen mask and switched it with the other one. He began pumping oxygen to Kaitty's lungs. They pulled into the emergency entrance. Kaitty was quickly rolled into the ER. Edmund tried to follow.

"I'm sorry, Sir, but you can't go back there," said a female nurse.

"But that's my wife! I have to be with her!"

"I'm sorry, Sir. It's our policy. You can wait in this family waiting room for updates on your wife." She led him into a small, enclosed room. He sat in a chair as the woman left and prayed silently.

God, don't let her die!

Several hours later

A doctor came in and woke Edmund. "Are you Edmund Lorenz?"

"Yes." He stood up. "My wife, is she alright?"

The doctor gestured to the chairs and they sat. "You're wife was in critical condition when she arrived—."

"Oh no," breathed Edmund.

"—but she will live."

He looked up to the doctor. "She's alive?" The doctor nodded. "What about the baby?"

"The fetus—."

"Please, don't call it that."

"I'm sorry. The baby sustained minor injuries. Even though there were many blows to the stomach, I think the baby will be fine."

"What blows? What do you mean?"

"Mr. Lorenz, your wife was hit and kicked in the stomach many times. It may have been an attempt to kill the fet—I mean the baby."

"How do you know?"

"There are bruises all across her stomach. Once your sister was able to talk, we asked her about them. She told us she thought the two men had hit your wife. We checked the baby by ultrasound and checked for bleeding. Miraculously, there was no bleeding and the baby looks fine."

"Wasn't she able to answer questions?"

"Mr. Lorenz, she's been unconscious since she arrived. The bullet wound to the chest probably caused this."

"How soon will she wake?"

"I'm not sure. But we were able to remove the bullets and stitch the wounds with no problems. Our biggest concern right now is that she might go into a coma."

"What—what could happen if—?"

"No one can know for sure. If she does not improve and is in a coma, the baby will be at high risk. C-section may be too dangerous for both mother and baby, but that may be all the chance the baby has."

"So, I could end up losing both of them?" The doctor nodded grimly. "But I can't lose them! I haven't even met my little baby yet. And to possibly lose Kaitty—."

"Remember, that may not happen. She could pull through."

"Can I see her?"

"Of course." The doctor led the way to the ICU. Kaitty was on the second floor.

When Edmund saw her, he wanted to cry for her. She was unconscious, an oxygen mask over her nose and mouth, an IV line in her hand, and a heart monitor attached to her. He stepped next to the bed. Pulling up a chair, he sat there with her. He reached out his hand and held hers tight in his. He prayed again.

God, please, let her wake.

Kaitty was in a daze. She had no idea where she was or what was happening. Her eyes were closed, but she could see three people. She was tied up, kneeling in front of two men with guns. The trigger was pulled and she was shot, dying.

She screamed. Could anyone hear her? Was there anyone around to save her? Or was she going to die where she lay?

No, Kaitty. You've got to fight! You've got to stay awake! Come on! Wake up!

And there he was, in her mind. She saw Edmund's face, sad and lonely. She couldn't give up. She had to wake.

Edmund watched Kaitty toss her head from side to side, wondering if it was a sign that she was waking. Or what if it was a seizer? She then emanated an ear piercing scream that made him jump. He stood up and leaned over her, trying to wake her from what seemed to be a horrific dream.

She began to cry and say, "I'm dead! I'm dead! Why, God? Edmund!"

"Honey, I'm right here. It's me, Edmund. Hon, wake up."

Kaitty continued to toss her head and cry, now saying, "I won't leave Edmund. He's my life. I can't die. God, please send me back!"

"You've gone nowhere, Kaitty." She wouldn't stop. Edmund ran over to the doorway and called out. "I need a doctor in here!" He went back to Kaitty and sat on the bed with her. Her eyes opened and she looked up at him. She sat up and threw her arms around him.

Edmund held her close as the doctor came running in. "What happened?"

"I don't know," said Edmund as Kaitty wept in his arms.

He got himself all the way onto the bed, leaned against the headboard, and let Kaitty rest in his arms. Soon she had cried herself to sleep. He didn't mind it. He relaxed and fell asleep as well.

Edmund woke at nine the next morning. Kaitty was still asleep, but he managed to set her slowly back down in bed when he got out. She rolled on her side and slept. He decided he would wait for her to wake herself.

He went out to the information desk on that floor and asked the nurse if they had the day's paper. The nurse handed him the *Omaha Times* newspaper and told him the doctor would be in soon to check on Kaitty. He nodded and headed back to the room.

He sat down in the chair next to Kaitty's bed and unfolded the newspaper. His mouth must have dropped open when he'd seen the front page. At the top were pictures of Hedrick, Andy, Kaitty, and Jana. He began to read the article:

Two Kidnappers, Two Hostages

Yesterday, the hide out of two kidnappers was found along with the two women who were taken from their homes. Jana Lorenz of Council Bluffs and Kaitty Lorenz of Red Oak were found in the living room of the kidnapper's hide out, shot, and unconscious. Both are hospitalized at the St. Joseph hospital in Omaha in the ICU. Jana Lorenz received a bullet wound to the lower left side of her stomach. Kaitty Lorenz received two bullet wounds; one to the right shoulder and one in the chest. Doctors tell us that there was a chance that she could be in a coma. There would be very little chance of the baby surviving a C-Section if it were necessary. Aside from this, she also has a broken right leg.

Hedrick Lorenz and Andy Hander where arrested on the scene after police had broken down the front door to gain entry when they heard shots being fired. Lorenz and Hander were accused of shooting Kaitty and Jana Lorenz and beating up on Kaitty Lorenz, punching and kicking her in the stomach and face several times. Hander could be sentenced to life in prison with no parole or death for sexual assault in the second degree, battery in the first degree, murder in the first, kidnapping in the second, aiding and abetting, and resisting arrest. Not all charges are related to this crime. Lorenz could be sentenced to twenty years in prison for kidnapping in the second degree, battery in the first, and resisting arrest. No court date has been set yet, due to the fact that Kaitty Lorenz will not be out of the hospital for awhile.

Jana Lorenz will be released from the hospital by Friday, but Kaitty Lorenz will stay longer until doctors are sure that she is of good health, assuming that there is no coma. Doctors say that she is in critical but, so far, stable condition.

Edmund couldn't believe it. First, his uncle and Hander were to be in prison, and second, two newspapers in a row had something interesting in them.

Someone walked into the room. "How's the patient doing?"

Edmund looked up and saw the doctor walking toward them. "Still sleeping."

"Have you found out what it was about—her yelling things, that is."

"No, not yet. When she wakes I'll ask her if she remembers it. I'll tell you anything I find."

The doctor nodded and left the room. Kaitty moaned and opened her eyes.

"Morning, sleepy head." He removed the oxygen mask from her.

"Morning. What time is it?"

"Only about half-hour after nine. You feeling okay? You need anything?"

"All I need is some food. I haven't had anything for two days as you probably know."

Edmund smiled and called for a nurse. The nurse came in and Edmund asked if Kaitty could get something to eat. The nurse nodded and asked what Kaitty wanted. "Anything that's food," she answered. The nurse smiled and said she would be back soon with something for her.

The nurse came back about ten minutes later with a tray full of toast with jam, eggs, bacon, and orange juice. Kaitty thanked her, prayed, and then ate. All her food was gone in less than five minutes. Edmund thought this was the perfect time to bring up the question.

Edmund leaned forward in his chair. "Kaitty, what happened last night?"

Kaitty put the empty glass back on the tray and looked to him. "I was—dreaming, I guess you could say, that I was back at that house. I was in the living room and he shot me. I thought I was dying and that I would never see you again. I was pleading with God, asking him to send me back to you. Edmund—it was all so scary." She began to cry again.

Edmund got up in the bed with her again and held her in his arms. Oh how he wished he could do more to comfort her. And there was a knock on the door.

Edmund got out of bed and went to open it. A nurse and Jana appeared behind it. "Jana." he said. They hugged. "You look much better."

"Jana wanted to see Kaitty," said the nurse. Edmund nodded and let them in. The nurse wheeled Jana straight to Kaitty and then she told Edmund to call when Jana was ready to go back to her room. He nodded and shut the door behind her. He went back over to Kaitty and Jana.

"So, you remember everything now?" asked Jana.

"Yes. I think that bullet might've done something to make me remember."

"Then what's up?"

"The sky."

"So, what's down?"

She thought for a moment. "Hell."

They all laughed. "Not the answer I was expecting, but okay!"

"What was that supposed to prove?" Kaitty asked.

"That you could remember."

"What are you talking about?" Edmund asked through his laughs.

"Kaitty had memory loss while we were at the hide out. Hedrick beat her up enough that she lost her memory. Do you remember him first beating you up?"

"I remember everything," she answered.

"Are you up to talking about it?" asked Edmund.

Chapter Eleven

Kaitty recalled the whole incident, starting from when she was abducted to when they were found. It seemed so painful, Edmund thought, for her to retell this story. He was glad his uncle was going to be doing time behind bars.

She looked exhausted. Edmund told her to rest and take it easy. Lying down in bed, she fell asleep. He watched his sleeping wife as she rested. He hoped and prayed that she would heal enough before the baby came. She didn't need any more difficulties.

He had completely forgotten that he still hadn't picked his favorite baby names. He found a pad of paper and a pen and started writing down ideas. He wrote every name from the Bible he could think of that was a good boy's name: Joshua, Samuel, Isaiah, Jeremiah, Daniel, Joel, Jonah, Matthew, Mark, Luke, John, Timothy, James, and Peter. He looked over the list and crossed out some names. He looked over it again, crossed out more names. He finally came to his last two; Matthew and James.

Before he could decide which he liked the best, there was a frantic knock on the door. Edmund set down the pen and paper and stepped to the door. There stood a young man with a tear-stained face. "Anderson!"

Edmund pulled the sobbing Rob Anderson into the room. "I'm sure I'm probably the last person you wanted to see, but I need to talk with you about something."

"Of course, what is it?"

"You know Claire...I found out today that...I couldn't believe...I saw her kissing another man!"

Edmund sighed. This could not be easy on Rob. Edmund wished he would have told Rob about his fiancée sooner. "Sit down." Rob did and Edmund sat across from him. "Rob, I know I should've told you this before, but...."

"She kissed you, too, I know. When I confronted her she told me that she kissed you. Mr. Lorenz, I don't blame you, but, when she told me—I wanted to kill you."

"I wanted to kill her when she tried to hit on another man."

"Another man? She never told me there was another one. She told me it was just you and the guy I caught her with today."

"When we were done talking with the agent at the Center, you noticed how quickly she left? I followed her and saw her heading toward this man. I ran down there and pulled her away. I told her I would tell you. She swore that if I told anyone, I'd be sorry."

"Did you take her seriously when she said that?"

"No. But I couldn't tell you anyway 'cause I passed out. What happened when she told you?"

"I told her the engagement was off. She took off the ring, threw it at me, and marched away. Mr. Lorenz—."

"Call me Edmund."

"Edmund, I don't know what to do. I thought she was the one! The one I would marry, have kids with, and grow old with. I guess I was wrong."

Edmund thought for a minute. "How old are you, Rob?"

"Thirty."

"Well, I'm almost twenty-three and it's safe to say that I think I may have a little more experience in this department. Maybe I can help you.

"I didn't ask Kaitty to marry me until I was twenty-two. We got married when she turned twenty-one, and now I'm going to be a father. I was just like you before, though. I had tried so hard to find my Miss Perfect when I was fourteen that I never noticed she was right in front of me. I was so focused on this beautiful popular girl that I ignored the unpopular yet beautiful, Christian girl that I was assigned to do many school projects with. She was smart, pretty, kind, funny—everything a man should want in a woman.

"But I didn't realize what that popular girl really was. She went around hitting on all the guys behind my back. When I found out, I had been going out with her for two years. I broke up with her. I was always alone then, I never wanted to be around anyone. But Kaitty— she wouldn't leave me alone. It annoyed me at first, but then I realized that she was doing it because she cared about me, not because she wanted me for herself. It felt good to know someone would be there for me when I needed someone to talk to. She would tell me 'Even if it seems there's no one on earth that loves you, God will always love you.'

"I decided that God had sent Kaitty there for more than just healing. He sent her there to be with me forever. From that point on, I knew I had found the one, and I never went out with another girl besides her. She was and is a blessing from God."

There was a pause for a moment. "So, you do believe in that God stuff?"

"Yes, and I'm not ashamed of it. I know He's real. Can't you feel Him?"

Rob shook his head. "With all of this—no."

"Has there ever been a time when you think you lucked out? Like had an accident that should've killed you?"

"Well, there was this one time when I fell out of a tree. I hit a rock, broke my skull and my back. Doctors said I would never walk again and that I might become brain dead. I couldn't feel anything below my neck. Sometimes I couldn't feel my neck. Doctors said there was no hope for me. Then, when I woke next, I could feel and move everything. I had no pain and I could remember everything I'd forgotten."

"That's what I'm talking about! That was God! He knew you weren't going to be like that for the rest of your life! He heeled you! You're just too blind to see it."

"I'm glad this whole religion thing works out for some people, but it's not for me. I'm not like that. And, if there is a God, why would He be interested in me? I'm nothing special."

"Because He created you, He created everything! And He wants you to believe in Him, to follow and preach His Word. He loves you."

Rob stood and strode to the door. "Well, if He loves me, then why did He send Claire into my life?" And he stormed out of the room.

Because He promises a smooth landing, not a calm journey, thought Edmund. *Lord, be with him.*

At seven that night, Kaitty had woken a while ago and sat talking with Edmund. She looked uncomfortable, though she just laid on the bed. "Are you alright?" he asked. He sat on the side of the bed for the third time.

"I'm fine," she answered. "It's just a little stomach cramp."

"Are you sure? You look like you're in more pain than just a little stomach ache."

"I'm sure." Suddenly, she grabbed her stomach and sat upright.

"Hey, hey! What's wrong?"

"I—I think the baby's coming."

"I'm calling the nurse."

"No! I'll be fine. It's too early for the baby anyway." She now leaned against the back of the hospital bed, both hands on top of her large stomach. Edmund was reluctant. She wasn't telling him something.

"You're not telling me the truth. Now—." He never finished. Kaitty released a grunting scream of pain. Edmund ran from the room to find the doctor. Eyes were staring and following him as he franticly searched for the doctor.

There was the doctor, running toward him. "What's happened?"

"I don't know! I think it may be time!" They ran into the room. Kaitty was holding her stomach and crying in pain.

The doctor examined her. "She's in labor."

"No, it's too early," Kaitty protested.

The doctor ran from the room and returned moments later with two nurses behind him. Together, they wheeled Kaitty out of the ICU and into delivery room 313 on the next floor.

Two nurses ran around, hooking her up to a different heart monitor, IV drip, and giving her medication to ease the pain. One of the nurses checked to see how far along she was. To everyone's astonishment, she was the full ten centimeters.

Edmund stood by her side, holding her hand, while they waited for the doctor to return and wash before the delivery.

"This is it, isn't it?" said Kaitty. She was most defiantly in pain. "This is the start of our new lives."

Edmund bent down close to her. "Yes. And you are strong. You can get through this." He kissed her forehead. "And I'll be there every step of the way. We're in this together, babe. I love you."

Once the doctor arrived, he told Kaitty to begin pushing. She did for nearly ten minutes before the baby's head came into view. She pushed again and the baby was out.

The doctor announced, "It's a boy!" The newborn was swept away to be tended to. He weighed six pounds, twelve ounces, and was a healthy baby, despite being three weeks early.

"What are we going to name him?" Edmund asked.

"I don't know. I wasn't able to decide what name I liked the best."

A few moments later, Kaitty screamed. The doctor came over and examined her again. "Oh no."

"What? What's wrong with her?" asked Edmund franticly.

"She's having another baby."

"What do you mean 'another baby'?"

"Sir, your wife was pregnant with twins. The next one will be here within the next ten minutes."

Edmund watched as Kaitty struggled with the pain, the medication now wearing off. "Can't you do something to ease her pain?"

"The baby will be here too quickly for any pain medication. It will be gone in a few more minutes."

He told Kaitty to start pushing again. She did and within five minutes, a baby girl was born.

The second newborn was taken, like the first, to be checked. She also weighed six pounds, twelve ounces, and was healthy, just like the first.

The nurses handed the babies to Edmund and Kaitty. They seemed to sleep in their arms. Edmund looked at his new little girl in his arms and said, "Lilly."

Kaitty looked up to him and asked, "What?"

"Lilly. Her name is Lilly."

Kaitty looked back to their little boy and said, "Gabriel." This time, Edmund looked to her. "What?

You can name our daughter after me, but I can't name our son after you?"

Edmund smiled at his wife. He loved the names. Lilly and Gabriel it was. They switched the two and Edmund looked to his little baby boy. He opened his eyes; he had Edmund's brown eyes. Kaitty smiled and looked back to Lilly. "She's opening her eyes." They looked closely at her.

"She has your eyes," said Edmund. They looked at each other, smiled, and kissed.

Kaitty thought of everything she had been through. Her old life was gone. Everything that had happened before this moment was just a vision of the past. Though things would pain her sore heart for some time, she knew everything was going to be okay. She looked at her two precious babies and it struck her.

This is just the beginning.

Chapter Twelve

Kaitty and the twins were released from the hospital two days later. They knew it was going to be a challenge trying to take care of Lilly and Gabe at first, especially with Kaitty's broken leg. But they had each other, they had friends, and they had family. Christine offered to stay with them and help them for the first couple of weeks, but they politely declined the offer. It was great of her, they knew, but they wanted to try to do this on their own.

The biggest burden was on Kaitty. She had a hard time trying to navigate on crutches and she could hardly do anything without Edmund's help because of it. When one of the babies cried, he had to get them. When Kaitty wanted something, he would have to get it. And when she needed food, he would have to make it and bring it to her. She didn't like it, but he said he didn't mind.

Well, of course he would say that, she thought. *He's trying to be nice. I'm sure he doesn't really want to do it.*

Well, now she was hungry and Edmund had finally fallen asleep from caring for Lilly. *Don't wake him. You can do this on your own. You need to stop asking for help.*

And that was it. She slowly got out of bed, grabbed her crutches, and began to go downstairs. The doctors said she shouldn't attempt them while she was in this state, and Edmund said that anything she needed, he would get. But she was not going to have it. She wasn't a cripple and did not want to be treated like one.

She came up to the top of the stairs and slowly started to lower herself. At one point she was able to do this, but with having gone through the trauma that she endured and just having twins, it would be more difficult than before.

She lowered herself to the first step, then the next, taking each one slowly and carefully. She thought she had it going, but on the fifth one, she nearly lost her balance. She considered going back up into bed and starving for a bit, but she decided that she was not going to back down. She was going to do this for herself, to prove that she was not a burden.

Once she regained balance, she continued. Finally she reached the first floor. She took a sigh of relief and continued to the fridge. She pulled out a slice of chocolate cake and sat it at the table. This was her reward for making it all the way down on her own—and of course for being hungry.

She put the plate in the sink and headed back to the stairs. Time for round two.

I've got it down, she thought. Half way up the stairs, her crutch missed and she fell backward down the stairs. She stopped at the bottom and the crutches came down on top of her. She didn't have enough time to cover her face. The crutches struck her. She let out a yelp.

Edmund woke from his short lived sleep to a loud thud. Then a scream made him throw off the covers and go running. He looked down from the top of the stairs and saw Kaitty lying on the floor, covered by the crutches.

"Kaitty! What happened?" He rushed to her aid, pulling the crutches from on top of her. "Why were you on the stairs? You know what the doctor said!"

"I—was sleep walking. I'm sorry."

He ran a hand through his brown hair. Sleep walking and yet she remembered the crutches? Something was up, but he didn't want to start discussing then. "Alright, let's get you back to bed."

Reluctant on the inside, she let him guide her up the stairs. She hated lying to him, but she didn't want him to know the truth.

They reached the top and Gabe started crying. "Sounds like it's feeding time. Can you make it back to bed alright?"

She nodded. There he went again, babying her. She tried to not show that she was upset and hurried off to bed.

A minute later, Edmund came in carrying Gabe. Kaitty held him and began to nurse him.

"You alright, babe?" Edmund asked after he climbed back into bed.

She nodded.

"Did you get hurt from the fall?"

She shook her head.

"Come on, babe, I know you better than you think. What's wrong?"

"Nothing. I'm tired. I want to go to bed."

"You want me to get a bottle for him?"

"No. I'm fine. I'll wait until he's done."

He sighed. "Alright. Wake me when he's done." He laid down to sleep some more.

Well, that was only part a lie. She looked down at her little baby in her arms. She smiled at the thought of this being *her* child, her own precious gift. Then she felt her casted leg bump the other. Why did it have to be her? Why was she the one who had to have a broken leg? She was independent and didn't want someone to wait on her hand and foot. It wasn't the kind of person she was.

New life indeed.

Gabe looked like he was finished for the night. Kaitty nudged Edmund to wake him.

He sat up. "He's done?"

Kaitty nodded. Edmund flipped the covers off of himself, trudged over to Kaitty's side, and scooped the baby into his arms. He carried Gabe back to his crib.

The next morning, Edmund went out to the grocery store to pick up a couple of things. He was reluctant to leave Kaitty alone with the twins, even for a little bit.

"Ed, I have to get used to taking care of them," she said. "You'll only be gone for half-an-hour. I think I can survive."

"Alright." He leaned in and kissed her. He left.

Now it was time to prove to herself, and to Edmund, that she could do this. She had to be able to navigate those stairs before Edmund would ever treat her the same. *Time to practice.*

She walked out of their room and up to the top of the stairs. *The easy part,* she thought. *Okay, Kaitty. Just take it slow. Don't rush.*

Step by step, she carefully mastered each step. Once she reached the bottom, she turned around and began to climb them. *Don't go too fast. Watch your balance and where you place your crutches.*

She was full of glee when she reached the top. She continued this practice for awhile until Lilly started crying. Should she dare try to carry her precious baby with one arm? She was frightened, almost to the core, but she had to do something. Lilly needed her, and she need to prove to herself that she could do these things.

She came up to Lilly's crib, set one crutch down, and scooped the screaming child into her arm. Carefully she sat in the rocking chair and sat down her other crutch. She had done it. She proved to herself that she was a strong person capable of these small tasks, even if this situation was temporary.

Kaitty nursed her little baby. She still could not believe that this wasn't any baby, it was *her* baby. This miracle was hers. She remembered when Anthony was born. It was amazing to see that new baby, but it was even better when that little baby was your own. She wondered how many God would give her. She loved them so much, but what if He didn't want her to have any more? It would tear her apart.

Why was she thinking of having more children already? She just had two when expecting only one! She shouldn't worry about what may happen in a couple of years. She needed to enjoy what she had right now.

Kaitty didn't tell Edmund of what she was doing while he was away, mostly because he never asked. But she wouldn't tell either way.

That next day he had to meet with the head Commanders of his base to discuss a few things. Kaitty took it to her advantage to practice more, this time on the basement stairs. Laundry needed to get done and she didn't want to wait for Edmund to insist on doing it.

She carefully took on each step, one by one. *Piece of cake!* The biggest thing that worried her was that she could slip up easier because the steps were not closed on the back side. One of her crutches could easily fall through and many things could happen.

She tried to push those thoughts from her head. She slowly made her way down. She made it. Now it was time to tackle the pile of laundry.

"Well, Captain Lorenz, it looks like this might take longer than an hour," said Commander Arthur Douglas. "Would it be alright if we talk longer?"

"Certainly," replied Edmund. "Let me call my wife and let her know real quick so she doesn't worry." He pulled out his phone and dialed.

Gabe started crying.

Kaitty tried to manage the stairs faster, but without luck. Just like she feared, her crutch slipped and she tumbled back down the stairs. She hit her back and head against the concrete. What she didn't know was that she accidently bumped a shelf too hard. It collapsed on top of her. Heavy objects pinned her against the floor.

Gabe continued to cry. She heard her phone ring. The one time she didn't have it and needed it.

She was scared.

"No answer." Edmund closed the phone. "She may be taking care of one of the twins. I'll call again in a few minutes. So, back to business, how long are we talking?"

"We're not sure," Commander Douglas said. "A year to eighteen months possibly?"

"What? My wife just had twins and you want me away from them for a year?"

"I know, Captain, but you have to."

"But my wife and kids. What will they do? What will happen to them?"

"Those are personal matters, Captain. But we can see what we could do."

"They can't just be left alone. She wouldn't be able to handle that!"

"I understand your concern, but you will have to leave."

Edmund nodded grimly. He checked his phone. Still no call.

Ten more minutes passed by and there was still no call from Kaitty. "I'm sorry, Commanders, but I need to make sure nothing is wrong at the house." He stepped away for a minute and called Kaitty again. Still no answer. He headed back over to the table.

"I'm sorry, but my wife's not answering her phone and I'm worried that something might be wrong. We're going to have to discuss more later. I'll be in touch."

He had to rush home. If something was wrong, he would never forgive himself.

Kaitty heard the front door open and close. "Kaitty?"

"Edmund! Down here!"

Feet ran across the floor above her. The basement door flew open and Edmund came bounding down. "Kaitty, are you alright?"

He pushed all the contents off of her and helped her stand up. "Why are you down here? And don't tell me you were 'sleep walking' again. You know what—."

"Yeah, I know what the doctor said. But I wanted to do it."

"Why? Do you know what could've happened? Why'd you do it?"

"Because I don't like being treated like a cripple! I wanted to do something on my own. I didn't want you to feel like I was a burden."

"Honey, you could never be a burden to me. I love you, I always have and I always will. Why don't you know that?"

"How would you feel if you had a broken leg, two babies, and an exhausted husband serving your every wish? Wouldn't you feel like a burden?"

"I guess, but, honey, I don't mind doing these things. I love doing them because I know I'm providing for my family. Everything is going to be alright. Let's get you upstairs."

That night, Edmund finally got Lilly to sleep. He climbed into bed next to Kaitty and held her close.

"So what do you think? Should we have another—but this time shoot for only one?"

Kaitty laughed. "Ed! I'm nowhere near ready to have another."

"I know. But don't you want to have another in a couple of years?"

"Well, of course I do. You know that I've always wanted a big family."

"I know. I just pray that next time you don't get kidnapped."

They laughed. "Or shot or beaten." They laughed harder.

Edmund's sides hurt. Even though it wasn't funny when it had happened, it sure was now. He hugged Kaitty and kissed her goodnight.

He thought of the conflict they had gone through that day. Little did Kaitty know that there was conflict rising.

Edmund didn't know how he was going to handle this one.

About the Author

Mysti Rolenc is a 14-year-old homeschooler. She started the *Kaitty Lorenz* series when she was only 12 and is currently working on the second book.

Mysti says, "I believe we're all given our talents to serve God. That's what I want to do with this series, to tell a story that revolves around faith in Jesus Christ."

She lives in Iowa with her family.

CPSIA information can be obtained at www.ICGtesting.com
Printed in the USA
241220LV00002B/373-555/P